Bullets

D1408068

& Blades

A Montague and Strong Detective Agency Novel

By

Orlando A. Sanchez

"I don't believe an accident of birth makes people sisters or brothers. It makes them siblings, gives them mutuality of parentage. Sisterhood and brotherhood is a condition people have to work at."-Maya Angelou

Thank You!

If you enjoyed this book, would you please help me by leaving a review at the site where you purchased it from? It only needs to be a sentence or two and it would really help me out a lot!

All of My Books

The Warriors of the Way
The Karashihan* • Spiritual Warriors • The Ascendants • The Fallen Warrior • The Warrior Ascendant • The Master Warrior

John Kane
The Deepest Cut* • Blur

Sepia Blue
The Last Dance* • Rise of the Night

Chronicles of the Modern Mystics
The Dark Flame • A Dream of Ashes

Montague & Strong Detective Agency
Tombyards & Butterflies• Full Moon Howl•Blood Is Thicker• Silver Clouds Dirty Sky • Homecoming• NoGod is Safe•The Date•The War Mage • Dragons&Demigods

Night Warden
Wander

Books denoted with an asterisk are FREE via my website.

www.OrlandoASanchez.com

ART SHREDDERS

No book is the work of just one person. I am fortunate enough to have an excellent team of readers and shredders who give of their time and keen eyes to provide notes, insight, and corrections. They help make this book go from good to great. Each and every one of you helped make this book fantastic.

THANK YOU

Amanda H. Amy R. Andrew W. Audra V. M. Audrey C. Barbara H. Bennah P. Beverly C. Bobbi M. Brandy D. Brenda Nix L. Carrie Anne O. Cassandra H. Chris C II. Chris H. Corrine L. Daniel P. Darren M. David M. Davina N. Dawn McQ. M. Denise K. Donna Y. Hal B. Helen D. Helen V. Jan G. Jen C. Jim S. Joscelyn S.

Karen H Karen H. Kevin M. Kimbra S. Kirsten B.W. Klaire T. Larry Diaz T. Laura Cadger R. Laura T. Lesley S. Liz C. MaryAnn S. Marydot Hoffecker P. Melissa M. Mike H. Natalie F. Nick C. Noah S. RC B. Rene C. Samantha L. Sara Mason B. Shanon O.B. Shawnie N. Stacey S. Stephanie C. Steve W.W. Sue W. Tami C. Tammy Ashwin K. Tammy T. Tehrene H. Terri A. Thomas R. Tommy O. Tracey M.C. Wendy S. Zak K.

<u>ACKNOWLEDGMENTS</u>

I'm finally beginning to understand that each book, each creative expression usually has a large group of people behind it. This story is no different. So let me take a moment to acknowledge my (very large) group:

To my Tribe: You are the reason I have stories to tell. You cannot possibly fathom how much and how deep I love you all.

To Lee: Because you were the first audience I ever had. I love you sis.

To the Logsdon family: JL your support always demands I bring my A-game and produce the best story I can. I always hear: "Don't rush!" in your voice.

L.L. (the Uber Jeditor) your notes and comments turned this story from good to great. I accept the challenge!

Your patience knows no bounds. Thank you both.

Arigatogozaimasu

The Montague & Strong Case Files Group AKA- The MoB(The Mages of BadAssery)

When I wrote T&B there were fifty-five members in The MoB. As of this release there are 810 members in the MoB. I am honored to be able to call you my MoB Family. Thank you for being part of this group and M&S. You each make it possible.

THANK YOU.

WTA-The Incorrigibles

JL,BenZ, EricQK, S.S.,

They sound like a bunch of badass misfits because they are. My exposure to the slightly deranged and extremely deviant brain trust that you are made this book possible. I humbly thank you and…it's all your fault.

The English Advisory

Aaron, Penny, Carrie

For all things English..thank you.

DEATH WISH COFFEE

This book has been powered by DeathWish-Thank you!

Is there any other coffee on the face of the earth that can compare? I think not.

To Deranged Doctor Design

Kim. Darja, Milo

You define professionalism and creativity.

Thank you for the great service and amazing covers.

YOU GUYS RULE!

<u>To you the reader</u>:

Thank you for jumping down the rabbit hole with me. I truly hope you enjoy this story. You are the reason I wrote it.

ABOUT THE AUTHOR

Orlando Sanchez has been writing ever since his teens when he was immersed in creating scenarios for playing Dungeon and Dragons with his friends every weekend. An avid reader, his influences are too numerous to list here. Some of the most prominent are: J.R.R. Tolkien, Jim Butcher, Kat Richardson, Terry Pratchett, Christopher Moore,Terry Brooks, Piers Anthony, Lee Child, George Lucas, Andrew Vachss, and Barry Eisler to name a few in no particular order.

The worlds of his books are urban settings with a twist of the paranormal lurking just behind the scenes and generous doses of magic, martial arts, and mayhem.

Aside from writing, he holds a 2nd and 3rd Dan in two distinct styles of Karate. If not training, he is studying some aspect of the martial arts or martial arts philosophy.

Please visit his site at OrlandoASanchez.com for more information about his books and upcoming releases.

ONE

"NOW? WHAT DO you mean now?" I asked.

"Now." Monty looked at Roxanne. "As in, where are my clothes?"

"I guess putting down a Kragzimik doesn't earn us a month or year off?" I asked. "It's not every day we have to deal with dragons, you know."

"Thankfully," Monty answered. "And the Kragzimik was a few weeks ago."

"Really? Felt like yesterday."

"We've been running these tests and the conclusion is the same. I have to wait it out. Now, my clothes?"

Roxanne pointed to the suit hanging in the closet on the other side of the room. The energy coming off her was a clear indicator she was displeased.

"Tell him you can't." Roxanne crossed her arms and stared at Monty. "You can't cast. I'll tell him if you won't."

"He's in trouble." Monty got out of bed and got dressed. "I have to help him."

"How?" The energy around Roxanne crept up a

notch along with the volume of her voice. "You *can't* cast, Tristan!"

Peaches rumbled next to my leg.

<I know, boy. She can be scary.>

<If I lick her, she will calm down. My saliva has healing properties.>

I forced myself to keep a straight face.

<How about you save that for later, when she doesn't look like she wants to blast Monty?>

<Can you make magic meat yet?>

<Working on it.>

<Good. I'm hungry.>

<When aren't you?>

<When I'm asleep.>

"Mages are trained to be effective even without magic," Monty answered, his voice taking on an edge. "Besides, I still have access to my magic and the Sorrows."

"Monty—?" I started. He gave me a look that said his mind was set. "Nevermind. Let's go see him."

"At the very least take this"—Roxanne removed a brooch and affixed it to Monty's jacket—"that way I know you'll be safe."

Monty looked down at the brooch and shook his head slowly. I looked over and admired the new accessory with an approving eye. It was a round red and silver Celtic design surrounding a trinity knot in the center.

"I have a shieldbearer," Monty said. "*You* should be wearing this."

"Inside Haven I don't need that many layers of protection."

"This is too much, and it will leave you in a weakened state," Monty said. "If I encounter any difficulty or incoming attacks, I can always use my shieldbearer *as* a shield."

"Tristan," she said, her voice suddenly hard, "wear the bloody bloom…for me."

"Fine," he said with a sigh. "Once my abilities normalize, I'm returning it. Understood?"

"Of course. In the meantime, keep it on."

I leaned in to examine the brooch. "That's pretty, and really brings out the color in your eyes, Monty." He shot me a glare. "What does it do?"

"It's called a bloody bloom, and it creates a personal shield." Roxanne adjusted it on Monty's jacket. "It won't stop everything but it's better than nothing. Which is what you have right now. No offense, Simon."

"None taken. Does it come with matching earrings?"

"We need to go." Monty grabbed her hands gently as she adjusted the brooch. "I'll be fine."

"You thinking that is what worries me." Roxanne squeezed his hands and looked at me. "You keep him safe."

I nodded. "He has me and my trusty, bottomless hellhound. We'll keep the destruction to a minimum, promise."

Roxanne crouched down and rubbed Peaches' head. "Simon, if his enemies find out he can't cast—"

"I know. I'll keep him safe."

"I'm perfectly capable of keeping myself safe, thank you."

Monty headed out of the room and to the elevators at the end of the corridor. I was about to follow when

Roxanne grabbed my arm.

"He is an obdurate, insufferable mage."

"You forgot slightly insane, tea-addicted, and short-tempered. Also, prone to massive acts of destruction. Should I go on?"

She shook her head with a sad smile. "Bring him back to me. He holds my heart."

I grew serious and looked down at Peaches. "We'll keep him safe."

I heard the elevator chime and Monty gave me a look that meant 'wrap it up or I'm leaving you' as he entered the car.

I half-jogged down the corridor and got in the car with him. Peaches bounded in next to me, and I heard a creaking sound.

<You need to go on a diet. The elevator can barely hold your weight.>

<Why is it my weight? It could be your weight.>

<It's your weight because you are the one on a steady diet of meat.>

<Meat is life. That word diet sounds painful. Will you go on a diet too?>

<Why do I need to go on a diet?>

<You are looking thin. Are you eating enough?>

<Of course I eat enough. We're not talking about me here.>

<If you ate more meat, you would be happier. That's why the angry man is angry. He only eats and drinks leaves.>

He did have a point.

Monty pressed the ground-floor button, and looked down the hall at Roxanne.

"You know she cares for you, right?" I said, as the doors closed.

"Yes. I do." He pinched the bridge of his nose. "It's just too complicated and too dangerous."

"I get it." I nodded. "What did Yat say?"

"Not much, he was being deliberately cryptic on the phone."

"This is Yat we're taking about. He's always cryptic. I think they record him for fortune cookie messages."

"You should share that with him. I think he'd enjoy that."

"No thanks," I said. "Not in the mood to get thwacked today. Pass."

We arrived at the ground floor, and the elevator slid open with another soft chime. I saw Yat standing in the lobby of Haven, looking out the window. He turned to us when he heard the chime of the elevator arriving and gave me a short nod.

I looked over at the thin, older man, and involuntarily winced when I saw him holding a staff. I didn't know how old Yat was, but he never appeared to age.

His slight build hid his immense strength and unbelievable speed. The last time I saw Yat, he wore his hair long. Now it was cropped short—a glowing white crown reflecting the sunlight streaming through the windows in the lobby. His eyes were still the same: deep, dark, and unreadable.

As we got off the elevator, I was looking across the lobby when I felt the shift in energy. Yat must have sensed it too because his expression darkened as he leaped over the furniture and headed our way. I pressed the main bead on my mala bracelet, pulling up my shield.

I turned fast and pushed Monty back into the

elevator.

"What are you doing?" Monty asked, stumbling back.

I grabbed Peaches by the collar and pulled him behind my shield as I backed up. The energy shift increased, and I felt a sensation like ants crawling on my arms.

"Yat has friends," I said, holding up the shield. "The angry kind."

Yat dived over a set of chairs and rolled into a crouch next to me. "Prepare," he said under his breath.

"Simon, don't be ridicu—" Monty started, when an immense orb of black energy crashed through the windows and exploded in the lobby.

TWO

"THERE ARE WARDS that protect this place." Yat moved from behind my shield to inside the elevator. "That should keep them out for now."

"Keep who out?" I looked around the mala shield. "Who's out there?"

I saw several bodies in the rubble of what used to be the lobby. The orb had converted the decorative stone and marble of the entrance into a blasted landscape of glass, stone, and debris. We were covered in black dust from the explosion.

"That orb…" Monty turned to Yat. "Who is after you?"

Peaches sniffed the dust-filled air and chuffed, shaking his head. The runes on the entropy stones of his collar gave off a faint red glow. I still needed to have a conversation with Ezra about removing both the collar and the matching bracelet I wore.

After Peaches' first and last obedience lesson, I was wary of heading back to the deli. Ezra was clever. It helped that he was the personification of Death. He'd

serve me a plate of pastrami and lull Peaches with a
bowl full of meat. Before I knew it we'd be in another
obedience training session, and the last one was enough
to deter any further hellhound training, at least for a
few decades.

<Something smells like home. The air smells bad.>

<Like home? You mean you smell dead people?>

<Yes. Dead and bad.>

"Something dead is out there. Which normally I
would say is impossible, but impossible left my
vocabulary long ago."

Yat looked at me suddenly. "How did you know?"

"There's something in this air." I waved the dust
away. "Something not all the way alive."

"You know this…how?" Yat asked slowly.

"He told me." I pointed at my perpetually hungry
hellhound of destruction. "I don't think we can go out
that way. Considering the entire front of the lobby is…
gone?"

"We can't stay." Yat looked around, pointing to the
stairwell off to one side of the elevator bank. "There.
We must go lower. It will confuse them."

I turned to Monty. "First responders will be here
soon. They'll think this is just an explosion, not a—"

"Magical attack," Monty finished with a cough.
"Roxanne will be one of the first down here. We have
to warn her."

Yat nodded and stepped out of the elevator. The
energy around the lobby dissipated. I tried to see who
or what had cast the orb. I sensed residual energy but
visibility was nearly zero because of the dust.

The stairwell door behind us burst open and

Roxanne stepped out into the lobby. Behind her, several men and women ran out wearing emergency gear. She narrowed her eyes and looked at us.

"Why am I not surprised?" She pointed at me. "Do you know how many renovations this facility has gone through ever since you two became regular visitors?"

Another group of first responders appeared, donned masks and made their way to the people trapped in the rubble. Roxanne approached us, her expression making it clear that she was willing to share ample amounts of pain.

"We just got down here," I said, holding my hands up in surrender. "Monty didn't have time to blow up the building. Besides, he's magically challenged right now."

"*He* can't cast. That doesn't mean you or your canine accomplice are incapable of wanton destruction." She narrowed her eyes and surveyed the damage. "We *just* had this lobby renovated."

Peaches nudged my leg, nearly catapulting me across the floor. I glanced down at him and moved to the side.

<What? I don't think you realize how strong you are.>

<If you ate more meat, you could be as strong as me.>

<Nothing can eat as much meat as you do.>

<The scary woman isn't happy. Is it because you broke her home?>

<What are you talking about? I didn't do this.>

<Everywhere we go, the places break or blow up.>

<That's mostly Monty…and you.>

<Maybe if you lick her, she will calm down?>

<If I lick her, I can guarantee that you will be out one bondmate. Trust me.>

"Yat?" Monty asked as we turned to look at him.

"What did this?"

"Yes, Yat," Roxanne said, her voice edging into lethal territory. "What destroyed the entrance to my facility?"

"My apologies," Yat said. "It was not my intention to bring this danger here."

"And yet here it is," Roxanne replied, waving a hand to indicate the damage. "Tell me what I'm dealing with, so I can reinforce the wards and direct my people."

"A Draugr," Yat said, looking at the remains of the lobby. "They are pursuing me."

"Joggers?" I asked, looking at Yat. "You pissed off mage joggers? Is that even a thing?"

"*Draugr,* not jogger," Monty answered.

"Since when do mages jog?" I eyed Yat, who gripped his staff in a familiar 'I'm going to whack you now' way. I took a step back. "Mages don't seem the athletic type."

"Revenants," Roxanne said with quiet menace. "You led revenants *here*?"

"It was not my intention," Yat answered. "I needed Tristan, and his energy signature led me here."

Roxanne stepped away and spoke to the group of first responders who waited for her. After instructing them, she whispered some words I couldn't make out. The next second, her hands were covered in dark energy as she traced some runes and touched sections of the wall. I noticed most of the dust recede from the lobby.

"Revenants aren't known for casting," Monty said, stepping close to Yat. "Who summoned them?"

Yat looked away. "Gabrielle."

Monty flexed his jaw, while taking a deep breath.

"Bloody hell. Is she alone?"

"No, she is not."

"And you brought her *here*?" Monty said, raising his voice. "Of all places?"

"I had no choice," Yat said quietly. "I was looking for *you,* and you were here."

It was rare to see Monty this agitated, which meant that whoever this Gabrielle was, she was a major threat.

"Why do you think I'm here?" Monty snapped. "I've had an accident."

"He can't cast," I added quickly. "Unleashed a neutralizer, crushed a dragon, and lost his magic."

"It's not lost," Monty snapped. "Just temporarily unstable."

"The Sorrows?" Yat asked. "Do you still wield them?"

Monty nodded. "This is also the onset of a shift. Casting could be unpredictable and dangerous, possibly fatal."

"Your inability to cast complicates matters, but does not change the present situation." Yat looked over the lobby. "We must leave this place before more arrive. I know where we can get help."

"Wait, that was just *one* of these revenant things?"

Yat nodded. "Gabrielle is powerful, but she can only command a handful of the casters."

"A handful?" Monty said. "She's gotten stronger."

"The longer we delay, the greater the danger. We must leave now."

"I agree," Roxanne said as she stepped up behind us. "Take the stairs and exit through the service entrance. That's where you left that thing you call a car."

"The Dark Goat is a work of automotive art," I corrected.

"The runes on that thing do *not* make it a work of art." Roxanne turned to Monty. "What was Cecil thinking?"

"A good question." Monty adjusted his jacket. "I still think he's punishing us for the London incident."

"The Urus wasn't our fault," I said. "I liked that vehicle."

Roxanne shook her head and placed a hand on Monty's shoulder. "Tristan, I don't recognize some of those runes on your new car, but the ones I do…is Cecil insane?"

"So far"—Monty rested a hand on Roxanne's—"it's kept us safe. If I notice anything out of the ordinary, I'll let you know."

"Please do." She turned to face Yat. "I don't want to deal with any more revenants. Keep them away from here."

"That's our cue," I said, opening the stairwell door. Monty and Yat headed downstairs. I was about to follow, when Roxanne put a hand on the door.

"Keep me informed about Tristan's condition. He's in the midst of a shift and dealing with the effects of the neutralizer. Things can get dangerous if he tries to cast before he's ready."

"Can *get* dangerous?" I looked around the obliterated lobby. "You mean more than this?"

"If Gabrielle is involved,"—Roxanne turned to the devastation in the lobby—"then yes. More than this."

I gave her a short nod and took the stairs to the lower levels of Haven.

THREE

I APPROACHED THE Dark Goat, given to us by SuNaTran, and opened the suicide door. Peaches jumped in, rocking the vehicle, but managing to avoid crushing Yat, who occupied one side of the back seat. Peaches curled up nicely on the remaining side instead of doing his usual sprawl.

<Nice of you to share your seat. Don't bite him.>

<I like him. He smells like those big yellow flowers.>

<Sunflowers? How do you even know what a sunflower is?>

<I eat meat, and meat makes me smart. You should eat more meat.>

I approached the driver's side and placed my hand on the door handle. The entire car flared bright orange for several seconds. I saw runes race along its surface and slowly fade away. I could see the smoke wafting up from its surface as the color fluctuated from deep purple to black, leaning more to the black.

Monty sat in the passenger side. Roxanne was right about a few things regarding the Dark Goat. The Pontiac GTO got its name from the Ferrari 250 GTO, a rare and beautiful piece of automotive art. The GTO stands for Grand Tourismo Omologato. I'm sure no one wanted to say that mouthful—so GTO became Goat, and a legendary muscle car was christened.

I adjusted my seatbelt and placed a finger on the dash panel near the steering wheel. The engine roared and settled into a purr, vibrating in my gut. Closing my eyes, I basked in the sensation and sound for a few seconds.

SuNaTran provided discreet service any time of day or night to any of the five boroughs and beyond—for a price. The transportation they provided—and I use the term loosely since each Rolls Royce Phantom was a tank disguised as a car—was the height of security, but there was a problem. The vehicles no longer appeared secure.

The Dark Goat was intentionally cursed. Cecil was having a bit of a PR problem with SuNaTran, mostly due to Monty and his violent friends. The last Goat, may it rest in pieces, was reduced to slag by a Ghost Magistrate.

I had taken a SuNaTran Aventador on a date. A troll had decided it would be better in small parts and attached a bomb to it, rendering it into Aventador art. It wasn't the only casualty of my date that night. Cecil wasn't pleased about that.

After what happened to the last SuNaTran vehicle we had while in London, I could understand Cecil's reluctance in providing us with transportation. SuNaTran's reputation was taking a hit, and he felt we owed him our assistance in restoring the company's tarnished name, considering we were the ones doing the tarnishing.

Enter the Dark Goat.

The runes that alarmed Roxanne were taken from another, darker vehicle, a 1970 Chevy Camaro dubbed the Beast. The thing killed its drivers. Something to do with the runic configuration and its disruption of life energies.

Cecil had tried, and failed, to destroy it several times. From what Monty told me, there was a Night Warden who seemed to have some connection to the cursed vehicle. He was driving the Beast. He wasn't immortal, but he was the only driver to survive driving that thing.

It was a win-win situation for Cecil. If we destroyed the Dark Goat, he would learn how to destroy the Beast, provided we survived whatever destroyed the Goat. If the Dark Goat withstood our use, Cecil could point to us and promote how awesome SuNaTran vehicles were.

<Can we go to the place?>

I shuddered, remembering our last trip to Ezra's.

<You remember the last time we were there?>

<Yes. He gave me extra meat.>

<Your recollection seems to be leaving out some of the more important parts.>

<Meat is the most important part.>

I shook my head. I could feel the waves of anger coming off Monty, sitting next to me. I adjusted the rear-view mirror, and saw Yat rubbing Peaches' flank and, surprisingly, keeping his hand.

"Where to? Or do we wait here to run over the revenant with the Dark Goat?"

"We need information," Monty said. "My knowledge of the undead is limited."

"Wordweavers," Yat said. "I must speak with Aria."

"I can't open a portal to her without considerable risk," Monty answered. "In my condition, we need an anchor. We need to go see Erik."

We pulled out of Haven and jumped on the FDR Drive. I headed downtown with a roar. The last time we saw Aria, we needed to use a portal from inside of Hellfire.

"Hellfire?" I asked. "I'm sure Erik will be pleased to see us."

"Yes." Monty nodded and traced a rune. "He'll know to expect us."

The rune blazed bright white for a second, before fading away and disappearing. "What was that?" I asked nervously. "I thought casting was dangerous?"

"It is," Monty said. "However, we can't just drop in on the Hellfire. Erik must be notified we are on the way. It's the protocol."

"What am I supposed to do if you blow yourself up while casting?"

"Spontaneous combustion is not one of the dangers," Monty said, rubbing his chin. "I would imagine self-immolation would be possible if I miscast a fire spell. If I attempt it, I'll inform you."

"How? By bursting into flame?"

"That would be a clear indicator, obviously."

"How about no casting until you get over whatever it is that's happening to you," I said. "Let's not blow up the Hellfire. Erik is going to be pissed seeing us as it is."

"You mostly," Monty said, pulling on a sleeve. "I think he still blames you for Quan."

"I'm going on the record stating I'm the least

magical, and therefore least destructive, one in this group." I pointed a thumb behind me. "Yat just finished destroying a lobby."

"Technically, that was the revenants," Yat said from the back seat. "You and Tristan manage to destroy entire buildings, from what I hear."

I glanced at Monty. "This is your fault. Your extenuating circumstances never seem to point at you."

"Guilt by association," Monty said, raising a hand in surrender. "Besides, I'm not bonded to a hellhound. You're getting a reputation."

"*I'm* getting a reputation?"

Monty nodded. "Everyone knows your creature is dangerous, it's right there in the name."

"Peaches?"

"*Hellhound*," Monty answered. "You do realize he's not just a large dog?"

"He's not dangerous."

"Of course not, as long as he doesn't grow to the size of a bus, shoot lasers from his eyes, or blink in and out of existence, all while being indestructible. Other than that, he's harmless."

"Exactly," I replied. "What are you going to tell Erik? Is he going to make the portal?"

"I'm in no condition to do so," Monty said. "I've never dealt with revenants, and Aria has the most extensive base of knowledge outside of Dahvina."

I glanced in the rear-view mirror at Yat. "Who is Gabrielle?" I asked as I dodged the yellow vehicles of doom—known as taxicabs in my city. "Why does she sound like so much fun?"

Yat let out a short sigh and briefly caught my eyes in

the rear-view. "Gabrielle is a necromancer."

"Like Beck?"

"No, Beck is a Negomancer," Monty said. "Negomancy is a discipline that negates magic. Necromancy deals with communicating with and summoning the dead."

"Wait," I said, swerving around traffic, "we're talking...zombies?"

"Close, but not the same," Yat said from the back seat. "Zombies do not cast magic. Revenants have been known to retain the abilities they had while alive."

"Undead magic-wielders. Wonderful." I switched lanes to avoid plowing into a new model carbon-fiber greenmobile. "Why not go to the Dark Council? Aren't they supposed to handle things like this?"

Yat remained silent and looked out the window. I glanced over at Monty.

"Yat chose to avoid the vampires," Monty replied. "It's a risk even seeing Erik."

"Excuse me?" I said, wary. "What do you mean avoid the vampires?"

"Revenants are undead," Yat answered. "They share a connection to other undead...like vampires."

"Are you saying Chi—?"

"Your vampire may try and stop us from destroying the Revenants—yes," Monty said. "You may need to have a conversation with her."

"A *conversation*? You mean have an actual conversation or an 'avoid getting shredded after several attacks' kind of conversation?"

"Possibly a bit of both," Monty said. "Probably leaning more to the latter."

"Oh, *your* definition of conversation," I replied with a shake of my head. "This just keeps getting better."

FOUR

THE SUN WAS setting as we approached the entrance to the Hellfire Club. I parked the car near the kiosk I'd used last time. I locked the Dark Goat with the usual clang and the orange flare of runes ran across its surface.

In front of the kiosk stood a woman dressed in a skintight black-and-white checkered costume. Her face was hidden behind a black mask. The mask was a combination of tragedy and comedy. She bowed with a flourish and twirled the pair of rune-covered tonfas she held when I approached. This was one of the Harlequin—protectors of the Hellfire.

She stood to one side of the large, rune-inscribed circle that rested at the top of the stairs. In order to get into the Hellfire, you needed to step in that circle—no exceptions. We stepped in. I took a deep breath, preparing for digestive torture.

"He's expecting us," Monty said with a bow, pointing to Peaches, Yat, and me.

The Harlequin returned the bow and slammed both

tonfas into the ground. The circle we stood in flared to life. A second later, we stood at the foot of a flight of stairs that led to a large wooden door. That was when the nausea attempted to remove my intestines, and my lunch threatened to eject itself. I hated teleportation. It always had the effect of twisting my insides out. Monty, Yat, and Peaches, however, looked unbothered. Clearly, I was missing something.

"Why does teleportation always hit me like this?" I groaned.

"Lack of focus," Yat answered. He gripped his staff, stepping closer. "Would you like some heightened focus exercises?"

"No, thanks," I said, leaning against a wall to recover. "I'm totally focused right now on keeping my insides… inside."

At the top of the stairs stood three Harlequin. Two of them stood to either side of the door. The third stood directly in front of it. Monty bowed to the Harlequin in the center. She returned the bow and waved a hand in the air.

"Welcome, Mage Montague," she said with a flourish. "He is expecting you."

"They need to do this every time?" I asked when my stomach calmed down. "Can't you flash some mage ID and just walk in?"

"No," Monty replied. "If someone were using an illusion spell to impersonate me, this is where they would be stopped…permanently."

The Harlequin weren't window-dressing. According to Monty, they were handpicked and trained by Erik into an elite security force. Each of them was an accomplished mage and could wield their runed tonfas with deadly efficiency. In other words, if you followed the rules, you left Hellfire alive; if you broke them, they broke you in several places and ejected the pieces.

We stepped inside and avoided the scenic route of dungeons and assorted BDSM-themed decorations. Prior to my first Hellfire visit, I had no idea mages were so kinky, but it made sense.

The magic they wielded required them to be in control all the time. It would only be an extension of who they were. Some needed to relinquish control and others, reinforce it. The Hellfire provided a much needed release.

A Harlequin led us to a large wooden door and opened it, allowing us to enter Erik's office. Another Harlequin standing inside closed the door behind us.

Two Harlequin stood sentinel, flanking the desk where Erik sat in an oversized chair. He was dressed in a dark suit, which mages seemed to favor, with a crisp blue shirt and no tie.

The office, though large, felt inviting. Bookshelves filled with books covered every wall. I looked around, noticing that the collection and the shelf space had grown even larger since our last visit.

Erik looked up from a pile of papers, frowning. He was clearly upset and it was easy to sense the tension in the room. He waved a hand, and the Harlequin left silently.

"Tristan, can you explain to me why I have revenants roaming the streets of my city?" Erik poured himself a small glass of the clear liquid he kept in a decanter on his desk and took a sip.

"We're working on it," Monty said. "I need a pocket dimension."

"Did you come all this way to inform me of something you can create with a gesture?"

"Under normal circumstances, I wouldn't."

"I have the Council all over me, asking for an explanation," Erik said. "In addition to revenants, it seems part of downtown has become a neutral zone."

"Peck Slip?" Monty asked. "About a block away from the river?"

Erik looked down at a map on his desk. "Yes, an entire block is now a magical null zone." Erik looked up and narrowed his eyes at me. "You two were there?"

"Possibly," I said, holding up a hand. "But it wasn't us. There was a dragon… a Kragzimik, or was it called The Kragzimik?"

Erik leaned back and steepled his fingers. "A *Kragzimik* caused the null zone? Is this what you're telling me?"

"We may have had something to do with that," Monty added. "We had to utilize a neutralizer."

Erik glanced up briefly and took a deep breath. "Oh, hell. A neutralizer? Do I even want to know *where* you got a neutralizer?"

"It all happened fast," I said quickly. "Kraggy was trying to stomp us, then Salao and George flanked us, and I had to deal with Karma, plus the drakes were all over the place, and the tigers, oh, forgot about the were-tigers, they raced in at the last moment with Dex and Kristman Dos."

Erik held up a hand, causing me to stop, and he looked at Monty. "You detonated a neutralizer? Inside the city?"

Monty nodded. "There were...extenuating circumstances. Death by dragon seemed imminent."

"How close were you when it went off?" Erik asked. "Were you in proximity?"

"I'd say very close proximity," Monty answered. "It was in my hand."

"That would explain the null zone," Erik said, rubbing his forehead. "The damage your agency causes in this city—"

"Is offset by the number of times we save it," Monty finished, with an edge to his voice.

"Just barely," Erik said with a sigh. "The Council mages had to contain the null zone before it spread."

"And I'm sure they did an excellent job," Monty said. "This would be a good time to create a new neutral location downtown. I hear Peck Slip has some excellent real estate."

"Droll, Tristan. How long are you out of commission?"

"Can't say," Monty replied, looking at his hands. "I'm told the effects are temporary."

"I truly hope so," Erik said. He looked over at Yat, giving him a slight nod. "Master Yat, to what do I owe the honor?"

Yat returned the nod. "I'm afraid I'm the cause of the revenant problem," Yat said.

"You're summoning revenants now?" Erik asked. "How powerful *is* that staff?"

"It's Gabrielle," Monty said. "And she's not alone."

"You mean she's with—?"

Yat held up a hand before Erik could finish. "Yes, he

is guiding her." He looked over at Monty. "After he abandoned his mentor."

"Shit." Erik downed the rest of the clear liquid in one gulp and poured another cup. "I really hope your condition is temporary because this is going to get much worse if *he's* in the city."

"He hasn't shown his hand yet," Monty said. "We may have time."

"The fuck he hasn't, Tristan." Erik polished off the second cup of liquid in one shot and gathered himself. "I apologize. That was crude and inappropriate. No offense."

"None taken." Monty moved over to the bookcases. "You're right. If Gabrielle is active, then he's showing his hand, and we need to act."

"I just remember the last time we dealt with him," Erik said with a slow shake of his head. "Having mages claw out their eyes, among other atrocities, isn't a scene I wish to revisit."

"Nor I," Monty answered. "If you recall, I recommended erasure or death."

"I recall the Golden Circle opting for tutelage and punishment, under the supervision of your brother, William."

"Killing him would have been more merciful," Monty said. "His discipline was uncontrollable, even with my brother guiding him."

"They weren't going to erase a Pavormancer. That discipline is rarer than Negomancy. They thought William could get his ability under control. They didn't count on his energy signature being so strong. He was a natural mage."

"William was a poor choice," Monty replied. "I remember his *lessons*."

Erik pointed to a volume in front of Monty, and it slid forward off the shelf into Monty's hands. "I'm sure he does as well. You sure you're up to this…in your condition?"

"I still wield the Sorrows," Monty said, taking the book. "It's not like we have much of a choice."

"That should get you started," Erik said with a nod. "I'm sure Aria has more."

Monty held up the book. "Thank you."

"Do you know what he's after?" Erik asked. "Besides killing everyone?"

"Immediately?" Monty looked at Yat. "Him."

"Yat?" Erik asked, standing and walking quickly to the other side of the office. "Why would he want you?"

"I am a means to an end," Yat answered. "The key he needs."

Erik stood in front of a large door and placed his hand on a panel next to it. "Yat, have I ever told you how aggravating your replies can be?"

With those words, I knew Erik had not trained extensively with Master Yat. That question would've earned me a painful introduction to his staff.

Yat stepped silently over the door and stopped about three feet away from Erik. "No," he said quietly, adjusting the grip on his staff. "Would you like to express your aggravation more plainly?"

Erik glanced quickly from the staff to Yat. "No, thank you," Erik said with a tight smile. He turned his hand, traced some runes in the air, and opened the door as they floated into the wood. "If I want pain, I'll step over to one of the dungeons. At least *that* comes with pleasure."

A gust of wind rushed into the office, calming down after a few seconds. "Pain and pleasure are both a matter of perspective," Yat said with a nod, crossing the threshold into the pocket dimension.

"How long do we have?" Monty asked. "I don't want to tax your anchor."

"The most I can give you is an hour," Erik replied. "After that it will retrieve you and send you to the neutral location near your home. The Randy Hump?"

"Randy Rump," I corrected. "It's the Randy Rump."

"I'm sure it is," Erik answered, giving me a look. "I have a meeting with the Council"—he looked down at his watch—"in about thirty minutes. Should I tell the Council Head you're on this, or would you like the pleasure?"

"We'll tell her," I answered. "Besides, I have a few questions about marking I need to ask her."

Erik shook his head. "Your funeral. I'll update her about the status of the revenants and *who* is behind this. You can tell her the *why* when you get back."

Erik motioned for us to step through the door.

"We'll speak in an hour," Monty said as we stepped through. "Thank you again for the book."

"Don't thank me, just get rid of the revenants before the Dark Council has to act," Erik said. "If we do, it'll be a nuclear option, and no one wants that, trust me. One hour."

He held up one finger and closed the door behind us.

FIVE

WE STOOD ON the summit of a mountain that was covered in grass and shrubbery. A few feet away I could see a pool of clear water. Next to the pool, a pathway led down the mountain. The woman sitting in front of the pool faced us but kept her eyes closed. This time I recognized the intense energy signature around her. Aria was one of the most powerful mages on the planet.

She sat in a lotus position, which I imagined was the standard wordweaver meditation pose. If I tried that, my legs wouldn't work for a few days.

"Welcome," Aria said. "It's good to see you all."

I wondered how she managed to *see* us since she still had her eyes closed. I was about to comment when Monty shot me a 'don't get us killed' look.

"Well met, Aria," Monty said, before I could say anything. "I need your assistance."

"I had a feeling I would be seeing you after the Kragzimik. Just not so soon," she said, opening her eyes. "Actually, I was expecting Master Yat."

"Well met, Aria." Yat bowed, placing his hands in a prayer position. "We need to speak."

"Is there anyone Yat doesn't know?" I said under my breath to Monty. "Do you think he's thwacked her with his staff?"

Monty delicately shoved an elbow into my ribs, causing me to wince in pain. "Can you try not to offend her?"

"What is he?" I asked quietly. "Is he a mage or does he just beat on them and their friends?"

"Yat is…complicated," he replied. "He wields magic in a unique way."

"I think the word you're looking for is painful," I muttered. "He wields magic in a painful way."

Monty nodded. "Occasionally."

Aria unfolded her legs and stood gracefully. Her long black hair cascaded behind her as she approached. She wore her usual white robe covered in silver runic brocade.

The silver brocade designated her level of power. After Dahvina, Aria was the most powerful wordweaver on the planet. Unlike Dahvina, Aria's eyes lacked irises, and shone with latent power, making her gaze unnerving at best.

She knelt and rubbed Peaches behind the ears, before looking in my direction and narrowing her eyes.

<Can you ask her to make magic meat?>

<I'll make some for you later.>

<You? Do you know how?>

<TK taught me the rune. It's just a matter of practice now.>

<Your magic needs a lot of practice. Can you ask her?>

"Aria, could I trouble you to"—I looked down at

Peaches, the hellhound equivalent of a sausage black hole—"make him some meat?"

She whispered into Peaches' ear, and he chuffed. A few seconds later a large bowl of pastrami materialized in front of him. Aria pressed some of the stones on his collar and nodded.

<At least say thank you.>

Peaches gave a low bark, nearly puncturing my eardrums. I winced and shook my head. Aria, unbothered by the ear-rupturing bark, stepped closer to me, pressing the section of the bracelet on my wrist that matched the collar.

"Two of your bonds are getting clearer." She whispered something I couldn't make out, and the sheath holding Ebonsoul disappeared along with my blade. "You need to keep that blade safe within. Not in a sheath, runed or not."

"What did you do?" I asked.

"What you were *supposed* to." She tapped my chest. "It's not far."

"The last time I tried doing that, I couldn't get it out."

"Your blade is a Seraph, among other things," Aria said. "Keeping it on your hip is dangerous. It will attract the wrong kind of attention."

"We aren't dealing with demons," I said. "I thought Seraphs were only attractive to demons?"

"You're dealing with creatures that will sense the power in the blade, and you. The properties of your blade have been augmented."

"What do you mean augmented?" I became still and felt for Ebonsoul. The current of energy was subtle, but present, very much like the bond I shared with Peaches. "It's in there, but I don't know if I'm going to be able to get it out."

"You need to practice," Aria said. "Besides, demons aren't the only entities to sense the energy of a Seraph. Once you materialize it, it will serve as a beacon, attracting good and evil."

Peaches gave a low rumble and paused in devouring the meat from the large bowl in front of him, which surprised me.

<*Practice is important. You should practice how to make magic meat.*>

<*How about you practice self-restraint? And maybe eat a little less?*>

<*I waited a long time before asking for more meat. I think that counts as self-restraint.*>

<*I would like to know what your definition of 'a long time' is.*>

<*The moment from when I eat meat until the next time I eat meat. That is always a long time.*>

I shook my head and adjusted the holster that held Grim Whisper.

"So now you're saying I've become even more popular with things trying to kill me?"

"In a manner of speaking, yes. Your energy signature is becoming more pronounced. This means you won't be able to hide."

"Hide?" I said. "I don't think you're using that word correctly."

Aria ignored my comment, turned and led us over to a small building near the pool. She sat on one of the ornate stone benches near the edge of the pool and looked at Monty.

"I take it this is not a social visit," Aria said.

"Some angry jogger tried to take out Yat," I said. "Monty said it was dead and you'd know how to deal with it."

Monty shook his head. "I don't have much experience dealing with the undead. Specifically *draugr* —revenants." Monty handed Aria the book Erik had given him. "I was hoping you had some information to assist me."

Aria took the book and gazed at Monty. A wave of blue energy raced across her eyes, lending an extra level of creepiness to them. "You're dealing with several factors at once," she said. "You're in the midst of a shift, and the effects of the neutralizer are currently making your ability to cast a potentially fatal proposition."

Monty nodded. "I can use the Sorrows as a channel for the time being." He looked down and flexed his fingers. I saw violet energy race across his hands. "That should help mitigate the fatal component."

Aria shook her head. "That will only be effective in low-energy casting," she said. "The moment you try something greater than a defensive spell or a teleportation circle, you run the risk of a runic backlash."

"I will make a concerted effort to channel any energy expenditure through the Sorrows," Monty answered. "The revenants aren't giving us much of a choice."

"The revenants are not your primary concern," she replied. "The one controlling them is."

Aria gestured with her hand, and two books

materialized next to her. She picked them up and handed them to Monty. I could see from their exterior and the yellowed pages that the books were ancient. I couldn't make out the titles, but judging from his expression, Monty was surprised to see them. He took them from Aria and opened the top one slowly.

"Ziller's Matter Theorems explaining binding and unbinding?" he said. "I thought every copy of this book disintegrated?"

"I had a word with Professor Ziller about practical jokes," Aria said. "These are from my personal library. Pay particular attention to the runes of undoing. Those should be the most effective in your use of the Sorrows."

"Thank you." Monty moved off to the side and began studying the books. Aria turned to Yat and gestured, causing several light blue runes to impact his staff.

"Several revenants attacked me earlier," Yat said. "I did not expect them so soon."

"Revenants?" Aria asked. "Does this mean you found them?"

"Some of them, yes," Yat said. "The revenants are being controlled by Gabrielle."

Aria raised an eyebrow, and I could feel the energy shift slightly around her. "Gabrielle? She never had the capacity to control revenants in the past. This increase in her power and ability is disturbing."

"She's not alone," Monty said, looking up from one of the books he was studying. "I'm certain Niall is directing her actions."

"The Pavormancer?" Aria asked, looking at Yat, who

nodded. "I thought he was confined by the Golden Circle? Are you certain?"

"Yes," Yat replied. "He is directing this attack."

"Niall?" I asked. "Who's Niall?"

"He is the one influencing Gabrielle," Yat replied. "A former student of"—he glanced over at Monty —"William Montague."

I turned to Monty. "Your brother?" I asked. "Dex said—"

"That he was a dark mage," Monty answered.

"Well, closer to: 'that one is black inside' or something like that," I said. "Sounded like William was bad news."

"He is," Monty answered quietly. "He went dark and took several mages with him when he left the Golden Circle. Niall was one of the youngest."

"We can say this Niall person's name now?" I asked, confused. "For a while I thought he was going to be the 'one who couldn't be named.'"

Yat gripped his staff, and I could tell he was edging closer to letting it do the talking for him. I moved away just in case he felt like focusing on me.

"This is a pocket dimension anchored in the Hellfire Club," Monty said quickly, before Yat communicated in his familiar physical way. "It creates a barrier between us and our plane."

"So, when we get back I *shouldn't* say his name?"

Monty shook his head. "I'd advise against it. Pavormancers have a unique sensitivity to their names being spoken. Names have power."

"Pavormancer?" I asked. "What exactly is a Pavormancer?"

"A Pavormancer is known as a fear caster." Monty closed the book that he held. "Do you remember the void passage?"

I nodded with a shudder. "You mean that wonderful feature of the Sanctuary?" I replied, as the memory gave me a temporary chill. "Worst fears, nightmares, and having your brain turned to oatmeal kind of fun?"

Monty nodded. "Think of a Pavormancer as a mobile void passage, except exponentially worse," Monty said. "They feed off your fear and then amplify it, creating a powerful illusion that feels like reality."

"This is what Erik was speaking about when he mentioned mages clawing their eyes out?"

Monty nodded. "The void passage is a weak simulation of Pavormancy. You've heard that there are worse things than death?"

I nodded. "Heard and lived it."

"Niall will make you wish for death. For someone with your condition, facing a Pavormancer would be deadly."

"Except, I can't—"

"For your mind," Monty finished. "He would destroy your mind while your body lived. You would be trapped in an illusion of endless agony for as long as you lived."

"Doesn't that sound pleasant," I muttered under my breath. "What does this Niall want? Do we know?"

Yat nodded. "Niall is looking to reunite the Hearts."

"Impossible. No one can reunite the hearts," Monty said. "The Black Heart is currently being utilized and contained in Fordey Boutique."

"True." Yat nodded and glanced at Aria. "The Black Heart is currently under the protection of The Ten."

"Good luck getting close to that," I said. "It's surrounded by a migraine field. Not to mention LD and TK."

"The White Heart was lost to time," Monty continued. "Last I heard it was frozen in a time loop and impossible to retrieve. No one knows where it is."

"That part...is less true. I have located the map to the White Heart." Yat tapped his staff on the floor and blue runes materialized along its length.

SIX

MONTY STEPPED OVER and examined Yat's staff.

"These runes…" Monty traced the symbols with his finger. He narrowed his eyes slightly. "These are *lost runes*?"

"Not any longer," Yat said. "Acquiring these nearly proved fatal. Gabrielle almost found them first."

Monty looked at Aria. "Did you know about this?" I heard the edge in his voice, it seemed like these lost runes were a big deal. "Do you realize the danger of these runes being rediscovered?"

I looked at Monty. "Can we not anger the super-powerful mage?" I said under my breath. "What happened to 'let's not offend her'?"

"You should heed your shieldbearer, mage," Aria answered gently, with an undercurrent of violence. "Do not forget whom you address."

Aria gestured with one hand. The runes from the staff flared bright blue and floated over to her hand, disappearing as they landed on her palm.

Monty looked at Yat and raised an eyebrow. "You're

working for her?" Monty asked. "Since when?"

"I did not realize I needed your permission to keep the world safe," Yat answered quietly. "Is there something you would like to know?"

"Monty?" Even I knew better than to piss off a super-powerful mage *and* a master martial artist semi-mage who wielded the staff of utmost pain. "Are we trying to get blasted here?"

Peaches padded over to my side and whined at me.

<The angry man feels wrong.>

<What do you mean, boy? Wrong how?>

<He feels dark, like the bad dogs in the place.>

Shadowhounds.

The memory of the wolf-like creatures made me shudder. Shadowhounds were created to neutralize and destroy hellhounds. Their fangs possessed a specific poison fatal to hellhounds.

<Are you saying you sense the bad dogs? Or Monty feels like the bad dogs?>

<The angry man feels like the bad dogs.>

I needed to keep an eye on Monty. There was a chance that the neutralizer and his current shift were affecting him negatively. I noticed that, ever since the lobby explosion, Monty was acting…*off*. He had ventured past irritating and had parked himself squarely in suicidal pain-in-the-ass territory.

Monty pinched the bridge of his nose. "My apologies, Aria," he said. "I've not been myself lately. That was uncalled for."

Aria looked at Monty and nodded. "I understand, you're still recovering from the effects of the neutralizer. I'm sure we have something to assist you."

"The lost runes were deliberately hidden," Monty said. "Uncovering them puts us all at risk."

"Would you prefer Gabrielle or Niall have them?"

"Of course not," Monty insisted. "I would prefer they remained *lost*. We don't know the extent of the power they contain. Especially not the central five."

"Tristan, don't be naïve. If Niall is looking for these runes, we must secure them *first*. Everyone is at risk."

The muscles of Monty's jaw flexed. I could tell that something was bothering him but he didn't want to go into detail for some reason.

"Don't you think having Yat find the runes poses more of a risk?" Monty asked. "This is power better left undisturbed."

"Yat is a man of singular talents," she said. "These runes are too important and dangerous to remain lost. He presented the lowest profile, making it possible for him to find these runes undetected."

"Is that why he led Gabrielle to Haven?" Monty asked. "His skill at stealth?"

Aria narrowed her eyes at Monty. Peaches gave off a low whine followed by a rumble. The energy around us increased in intensity and I prepared to be blasted into atoms.

"Monty, maybe we can discuss this when you're feeling—" I started.

"Lost runes are ancient magic, uncontrollable at best," Monty interrupted. "You know this, Aria."

"Or not," I said, stepping back and looking around for cover. If Aria decided to go on a rampage, we were done.

"No one has a working knowledge of these runes

being used," Monty continued, rubbing his left temple. "We don't know the extent of their power."

"*You* don't know the extent of their power," Aria said, looking at Monty and standing. "Please come with me. I'm concerned that your energy signature is fluctuating out of control. We need to get you to the infirmary."

"It's nothing," Monty said, waving her words away. "I'm sure it's just the effects of the neutralizer."

Monty took a few steps forward and stumbled before Yat managed to grab his arm and steady him, preventing him from falling.

"What's wrong?" I asked, worried. "Monty?"

Yat wrapped an arm around Monty's waist, and entered the small building beside the pool, following Aria. Peaches gave a low rumble next to my leg as we entered the building too.

<What's wrong with the angry man?>

<He's not feeling well.>

<If he ate meat, and not leaves, he would feel better.>

<Monty doesn't eat meat, it has something to do with his being a mage.>

<He'll feel better if I lick him.>

<Let's save your super saliva for an emergency. I'm sure Aria has something to help him.>

I noticed the door on the far side of the small building. Aria placed her hand on the center, whispering some words I didn't understand under her breath. A series of runes flowed from her fingers and the door opened inward, leading to a long, brightly lit corridor.

The corridor was featureless stone. I saw no distinguishing markers or symbols. We walked in silence for a few minutes. When we reached a T-junction, I looked left and right, noticing that all the corridors looked the same. A feeling of recognition came over me.

"What is this place?" I said, looking down the corridor we traveled. "It reminds me of the Corridors of Chaos."

Aria looked over her shoulder and gave me a nod. "It should," she said. "These are the original Corridors of Chaos. The ones in London are a smaller version of this network of corridors."

"You know about the ones in London?" I asked. "That was like getting dropped in a maze."

"I should, I designed them," Aria said. "These are considerably more extensive, with shifting and disappearing sections. Please stay close, getting lost here would make it nearly impossible to locate you."

I stepped closer to her, keeping my voice low. "What's wrong with Monty? Is it the neutralizer?"

"Back in Haven, was he hit by the spell that exploded in the lobby?"

"No. We had just come down in the elevator when it happened."

Aria glanced back and then looked at me, giving me a small shake of her head. "This is deeper than the neutralizer," she said. "It has to do with his shift. You're his shieldbearer. What do you sense?"

I let my senses expand, and tried to feel Monty's energy signature. Initially, I sensed his signature, but then it became garbled, overlaid by something stronger and darker.

"I sense his usual signature, but there's something

else." I shook my head. "It's something stronger, something that's not Monty."

Aria nodded. "Every shift a mage experiences is a risk." We reached another junction and she placed her hand on the wall, closing her eyes for a second. We turned left and continued forward. "During a shift, there are forces at play that can cause a mage to succumb to the power."

I glanced behind me and looked at Monty. Yat made sure that Monty navigated the corridors without falling behind. I didn't know what he was going to do, but I knew that Monty wouldn't go dark. We all had darkness within us, and it was something that we each had to battle on a constant basis.

"Is that what happened to William?" I asked. "Did he give in to the power?"

"I think you should ask Tristan about that," Aria said. "I will tell you that William was two shifts away from becoming an archmage. He possessed the power, ability, and force of will to execute dangerous and powerful spells."

I nodded. "You know Monty's not going to stop casting. Especially if the city is in danger."

"He's a Montague," she said. "You're his shieldbearer. It's your purpose to make sure he remains safe from danger. Even if that danger comes from within."

"Great. I get to stop the most stubborn individual I know from trying to use magic. That's not going to be difficult at all."

"If it were easy" —she placed a hand on my shoulder—"then anyone could bear the shield. You were chosen because you're capable. I do think you will face some difficult choices ahead."

We turned several more corners until I was thoroughly lost, and then we faced a large door. Aria opened it and we found ourselves inside an infirmary. Beds lined both sides of the room, along with short tables holding miscellaneous medical supplies.

There were also some instruments I didn't recognize. I figured these were specific to the wordweavers. A blue wave of energy raced across the floor when she closed the door.

She pointed to one of the beds and Yat helped Monty sit. She gestured with one hand while placing the other on Monty's forehead. Runes materialized on every surface of the room. The walls, ceiling, and floor blazed with symbols I didn't recognize. Monty closed his eyes and lay back in the bed.

"What was that?" I asked. "Is that like a Monty off-switch and, if so, can you teach me how to do it?"

"It's something to help him deal with the effects of the neutralizer," she answered. "I can help him mitigate the blockage, but I can't do anything about his current shift."

"What happens if he shifts but is still dealing with the effects of the neutralizer?"

Her expression became hard and she looked at me. "You must make sure that he doesn't embrace the power over his purpose. Do you understand?"

"Not in the least," I said, shaking my head. "I don't even know what his purpose *is*."

"You will," she said with a smile. "Now, you don't have much time before the anchor retrieves you. Yat will remain with you until this threat is dealt with."

"That's comforting," I muttered. "Is that really necessary?"

"It is," she said. Her tone made it clear it wasn't up for discussion. "You will thank me later."

Yat put his hands in a prayer position and bowed. "It would be my honor to watch over them."

Aria gave him a short nod. "In the meantime, I must attend to some urgent matters and ensure that these lost runes are secure. We cannot let the hearts be joined."

"Are there other lost runes?" I asked. "Will Niall be looking for them?"

Aria glanced at Yat. "Simon's right. With the other runes out there, you must secure the White Heart."

Yat nodded. "I have the location," he said. "It will be difficult to remove the White Heart from its containment."

"The alternative is annihilation," Aria answered. "If it cannot be retrieved, you must destroy it. There is no other option."

She gestured and materialized the books that she had given to Monty. Yat gave her a short nod and placed them in the pack he carried.

I wasn't overjoyed with the idea of being in proximity to Master Yat or his staff, mostly his staff, but I knew we needed help. If we were going to face undead creatures and a nightmare-inducing mage, I'd rather have him on my side.

SEVEN

"WE HAVE A few moments," Yat said. "Let's work on your flow."

Once I heard the word *flow* all my brain registered was *pain*. "Now?" I asked, looking at the prone Monty sleeping in the bed. "Isn't the anchor going to retrieve us soon?"

"Summon your blade."

I extended my hand and willed Ebonsoul to materialize. I stood there for several seconds, just staring at my empty hand, remembering my failed attempt in London.

"That would be problematic in a fight." Yat pointed at my outstretched hand. "Does it need to warm up first?"

"I knew this would happen," I said. "Now it's stuck inside. Last thing I need is for my blade to appear when I least expect it."

"It is not stuck, *you* are," Yat said with a small smile.

I groaned and held up a hand. "Before we begin— one question."

Yat nodded as he stepped over to the other end of the room and moved one of the beds to give us fight—*flowing*—room. He was a strong believer in the 'any place is a dojo' school of thought.

Converting the most mundane places into a training space was his special gift, and we had done this torture several times in the past.

His words came to mind as he cleared the space. *Fight everywhere, so you may always be prepared.*

"This will do." He removed the pack he wore and shrugged off his light jacket, placing them on an empty bed. "Please, ask your question."

"I've been near the Black Heart, and nearly fried my brain just standing in the same room with it," I said. "You're not a mage."

"Those are statements, not questions." Yat stood still, holding his staff vertically next to him. "Do you know the difference between the two?"

I nodded and took a breath. I realized early on that his responses were deliberately crafted to push buttons, and in my case, disrupt both my mental and physical balance.

"Yes," I said with a tight smile, remembering how close his staff was to my head. "My question is: How can you destroy the White Heart if you can't remove it?"

"Magic, spells, casting, are all different names for the same thing—energy and its manipulation," he said, and extended the arm holding the staff. "I may not be what you understand to be a mage or"—he glanced over at Monty—"a wizard. You will find that it is not the title that bestows power, rather the ability to alter and align to different frequencies that makes the difference."

He brought the staff close to his body, flicking his wrist downward as the staff became a silver mist and flowed into his palm, disappearing from sight.

"How did you—?" I shook my head, remembering Monty's words. *Yat is complicated.*

"Are you ready?" he asked, placing one foot slightly ahead of the other, turning the toes inward and bending the knees. A classic hourglass stance. "Let us see if we can coax your weapon out. Single arm, please."

"You didn't answer my question." I stepped close to him in the same stance, and extended an arm, palm facing me and fingers to the ceiling. I placed my other arm behind my back.

He extended an arm and mirrored my hand position, maintaining contact at the forearm right behind my wrist. He called this the bridge. I called it imminent agony.

"I did." He launched a fist at my throat. "You weren't paying attention."

I shifted my hips and rotated my torso away from his fist. Since we were only using one arm, I had to compensate, making sure I didn't lose my balance. Yat gave a short nod of approval and redirected his fist by rotating his wrist, opening his hand and slapping me in the face. Hard.

It wasn't a Karma-level slap, but I still saw bright spots from the impact.

"Feel for your weapon," he said. "It's part of you. Sense the bond you have with it."

I took a deep breath, let it out, and searched inward

for my blade. Yat attacked again, this time with a spear hand to my throat. I tucked my chin and redirected his thrust to the side of my head. His fingers grazed my ear as they shot past.

"You want me to sense the blade while you poke a hole in my throat?" I asked. "You're barely giving me a moment to think."

"Precisely," he said, peppering my chest with blows. "Stop thinking and draw your blade."

The percussive element of his strikes stole my breath, and I began gasping. Aside from feeling like a conga drum, his attacks were designed to capture my center.

The moment that happened, it was over. The centerline of the body was the most vulnerable, and as his attacks continued, I realized he wasn't holding back. This wasn't training, this was a fight.

I shifted forward, driving an elbow into his face. He bent back, dodging the strike and unleashing a low kick at my knee. I stepped to the side, avoiding the low kick and unleashing a fist.

Silver mist formed around his hand, and in a split-second, he materialized his short staff and deflected my fist with a quick blow.

"We're using weapons?" I said, surprised. "I thought we were working on flow. Just hands."

"*My* flow is completely functional, as you can see," he said, stepping back. "*You* are the one that is stuck."

I nodded. "Exactly. That's why we were using just hands."

"Do you think the enemies you will be facing will wait until your flow is established?" He shook his head. "It is precisely that state that they will exploit."

"It's these bonds," I muttered, more to myself. "They're entangled and make it almost impossible to draw my blade."

"It isn't the bonds." He leaned back into a fighting stance. "It is how you perceive the bonds."

I could feel myself getting frustrated at his response. "Do your answers ever help *anyone*?"

He nodded. "All the time." He thrust forward with his staff, striking my midsection and doubling me over. I rolled out of the way, catching my breath as he brought the staff down where my head was moments earlier.

He was serious. I calmed my breath and felt for the bond I had with Ebonsoul. It was tenuous at first, but it was there. I mentally reached for it, extending my arm as Yat slid forward with a horizontal strike.

A small cloud of silver-gray mist formed in my hand, solidifying into Ebonsoul as I parried the strike. Yat raised an eyebrow in approval, rotated his body faster than I could track, and slammed the staff into my legs, sweeping me off my feet. I landed hard on my back with the end of his staff pointing at my throat.

"You cannot wait until your life hangs in the balance to establish your flow," he said, extending a hand and lifting me to my feet. "It must become as easy as the breath you take."

"Right now, my breaths aren't coming too easily," I said in between gasps. "I felt the bond, but it's like trying to squeeze water."

Yat nodded. "Then do not squeeze."

"What does it do?"

"What does the Gray Heart do?"

I nodded, expecting an esoteric answer about moving the forces of the universe.

Yat frowned. "Both hearts are temporal runes given substance. To join them is to control time."

"Control time? For how long?"

"For as long as you wish. If you possessed the Gray Heart, time becomes irrelevant and no longer linear."

"Why do mages create these crazy items?" I asked. "Don't they read? The one ring, the super enhanced sword that cuts through reality, a crazy rune that can stop time…it always ends badly."

"Mages have power, and some of the mages in history felt a need to give that power expression," Yat answered. "In this instance, it was power wielded to form a weapon, as is usually the case."

"The gray heart is a weapon?"

"If you have a method to stop or control time, why would you need an army?"

"Good point."

"These lost runes are of the five," Yat said. "If we can locate them all, we can protect this and every plane."

"How many of these lost runes are there?"

"The central five are the most familiar," Yat answered. "But there are records of many more with properties we don't understand."

Aria came running into the room. "You must leave at once," she said, gesturing and forming a teleportation circle. "Hellfire is under attack. You must go there now. If the anchor is disrupted, you will remain trapped here."

I looked over at Monty, who was still unconscious.

"What about him?"

"I'm fine," Monty said from the bed, opening his eyes. "Thank you, Aria. That spell—"

"…Was a temporary measure, Tristan," Aria finished, creating the circle and placing a palm in the center. Orange runes raced around the edge, brightly illuminating the circumference of the circle. "You must not cast. Use the Sorrows, and direct your magic through them."

"I will," Monty said. "I have no wish to cut my life short."

"There's something else," Aria said. "When I cast the limiter spell earlier, I sensed a foreign energy signature. You must get back to Haven and let Roxanne examine you."

"Right now we need to make sure that the Hellfire Club remains intact," Monty answered. "If it's compromised, there are artifacts within its walls that can end us all."

We stepped into the circle. Aria gestured and traced runes in the air. The circle rotated beneath us and flashed bright violet, blinding me. There was no sensation of movement. I blinked my eyes several times, and when I could see again, I realized that we were back in Erik's office.

EIGHT

"WHO WOULD DARE attack Erik in the Hellfire?" I asked, looking around. "It's like they're asking to walk into a world of pain. And I'm not talking about the good pain that Erik keeps referring to."

Monty looked at Yat. "They're tracking you," Monty said with an edge in his voice. "How are they doing this? Considering your formidable levels of stealth?"

Monty was entering pain-in-the-ass territory again. "Monty, before we start throwing accusations around," I said, "how about we locate Erik and his army of Harlequin that seem to be missing?"

"I do not think I am the one being tracked," Yat said, shaking his head. "The shift you are undergoing is broadcasting your energy signature like a beacon. Tracking would be a simple matter."

"Are you saying that they're tracking *me*?" Monty asked. "My energy signature should be diffused due to the effect of the neutralizer. I highly doubt it's my energy signature."

"Erik?" I said. "Harlequin? Hellfire under attack?"

"I'm well aware of the situation, Simon," Monty shot back. "If I wanted a situational assessment I'd ask for one."

"Excuse me," I said. "Sounds like someone needs a hot cup of tea and a nap."

"You are not feeling well, Tristan," Yat said, materializing his staff. "We must secure this location, and then we can determine how they are following us. Agreed?"

Monty reached behind him and drew the Sorrows. A soft wail escaped them as he pointed them at Yat. Blue energy raced across their length, as the new runes designating them Seraphs pulsed a brighter blue.

"This has nothing to do with my shift, and everything to do with *you* uncovering lost runes."

"Monty," I said, "maybe you want to point the very sharp, dangerous swords away from the martial arts master?"

Monty whirled on me, and I took a step back. Peaches gave off a low rumble and took a step closer to me.

"Don't you *dare* tell me what to do," Monty hissed. "Do you know who I am? The power I possess?"

I took another step back. Mage megalomaniac was starting to creep me out. "Monty, it's me, Simon." I let my hand drift closer to Grim Whisper. I had loaded it with Persuader rounds, but the last thing I wanted to do was shoot him.

"Tristan, you are not well, you need—" Yat started.

I felt the wave of energy rush across the room and hit Monty square in the chest. He froze in place a second later.

"What he needs," a female voice said from behind us, "is to die."

Yat turned suddenly, his staff in a defensive position. "Gabrielle, what did you do to him?"

Gabrielle looked like she was on her way to a meeting. She wore an Anaste collarless leather jacket, with matching leather pants, and heels that could double as weapons on their own. Her platinum blonde hair flowed behind her, which I took as a bad sign since there were no open windows in the Hellfire.

Black energy raced across her hands and up her arms, and I felt like throwing up all of a sudden. I clenched my stomach. This was like using a teleportation circle, only worse.

"My stomach," I said with a groan. "What the he—?"

"I have that effect on people." She cocked her head in my direction. "You're interesting, aren't you?"

Yat stepped forward and caught her attention. "What did you do to Tristan?"

"Nothing really," she said with a smile. "He's just been exposed to obsidian dust. I hear it's fatal to magic-users."

The realization dawned on me. "The dust in the lobby," I said. "It was a setup."

"What do you want?" Yat asked, his voice hard.

"It's not what I want, it's what you need. Or rather, your mage friend.

"An antidote," I said. "You have one."

Gabrielle nodded and pointed at me. "You're brighter than you look," she said. "I do have one, and I'm willing to share it, once Master Yat points me in the right direction."

"The White Heart," Yat said. "You want its location."

"Either give me the location or William's little brother dies," Gabrielle said. "Your choice."

I thought back to LD and TK. "There's a way to get the poison out of him. But we need to get Monty to Fordey."

Gabrielle laughed. "By the time you do, you'll be carrying a corpse."

We were running out of options and time.

A creature came shuffling into the office.

All my ideas about zombies were dispelled in that second. This was a man with a grayish complexion dressed in what used to be a suit. His skin had turned purple in places, and a stench shuffled in with him, trying to destroy my ability to breathe.

His eyes stopped me. This wasn't a mindless creature wandering about. His eyes held intelligence, and something else…a pleading. He was being controlled against his will.

"Revenant?" I said, trying to hold my breath against the smell that suddenly filled the office. "I'm guessing tall, dark, and putrid is with you?"

"This specimen," Gabrielle said admiringly, "used to be a mage when he was alive. Now that he's mostly dead, I use him to deal with insignificant pests. Like you."

"That's some retirement plan you got there," I said, trying to buy some time. "Excuse me, while I throw up."

I had an idea. It was thin at best, but it was the only option we had, the only one I could see. If we couldn't bring Monty to LD and TK, we'd have to bring them to

Monty.

<Hey, boy, do you remember the scary lady that makes you the best meat?>

<The meat that never ends?>

<Yes. Do you think you could find her, the way you can find me?>

<Is she going to make me some meat?>

<If you can take us to her, I'll make sure she makes you the largest bowl of meat you can eat.>

Peaches growled, chuffed, and shook his body.

<I'm going to speak now. It's going to hurt your ears. Hold on.>

The rumble started deep in his stomach. I grabbed his collar as he barked and pushed off with his hind legs. Erik's office blinked out of existence.

NINE

THE NEXT MOMENT, I realized we were standing in the Hall of Ten, with a very angry-looking TK holding an orb of green energy in one hand and a long, sharp sword in the other.

"You are one second away from testing the limits of your immortality," she said. "Explain your presence here, now."

I stood in an open reception area the size of an enormous hotel lobby. A large, gleaming, golden X, outlined in red, dominated the center of the black marble floor. It reflected the light pouring in from a domed window set in the ceiling. I looked around, remembering the smoldering crater, that had dominated the center of the black marble floor, and the shattered domed window in the ceiling after Salao and the drakes had destroyed the Hall.

The Hall appeared larger than last time. The renovations had restored that sense of stepping into a large museum, removing the burned-out battleground look. White marble benches were situated along the walls at even intervals, with small recessed alcoves above each bench.

Intricately carved, white marble statues stood inside each alcove. All of the statues were in action poses except for one. I glanced over to that one and recognized the statue of TK.

Her statue stood with her hands resting on a sword, point down. Her legs were slightly apart, and the lifelike expression on her face was a cross between a scowl and a smile, as if to say, 'Step closer so I can shred you.'

I shuddered. The statue only captured a fraction of the intensity TK possessed. The intensity I was facing right this moment.

"Don't kill him, hun." LD stepped over and rubbed Peaches' head. "At least not yet. Let's find out why he would take on a suicide mission like breaching Fordey."

"He's here unannounced and uninvited." TK narrowed her eyes at me. "That rudeness deserves a stab at least."

"Monty's in trouble," I said quickly, aware of the fact that TK still hadn't sheathed her sword. "He inhaled obsidian dust, a necromancer set him up, now they want the White Heart, I left Yat alone with her, and she froze Monty."

LD held up a hand. "Slow down, hombre. Did you say White Heart?"

TK sheathed her sword and absorbed the orb of energy. "Where is Tristan? How did he inhale obsidian dust? He should have sensed it, even in his condition."

"They're at the Hellfire Club, and Monty is acting weird."

"Weird? How?" TK asked. "What are the

symptoms?"

"He's turned into a superior, condescending, arrogant mage of buttheadedness," I replied. "I mean more than usual."

"Have you met Tristan?" LD said as he began to gesture. "That's called normal for him."

"Not like this," I said. "The dust is doing something to him. Or the neutralizer and the shift are frying his remaining brain cells. He pointed the Sorrows at Master Yat."

"Oh," LD said quietly, shaking his head. "Maybe he is losing his mind."

TK nodded. "I've seen this before." She nodded to LD. "We're going to need the go-bag. Obsidian dust isn't as concentrated as the ice, but it can still be fatal."

"Who is the necromancer?" LD asked. "Did you see him?"

I nodded. "It's her, not him. Can we discuss this on the way?"

"No," TK said with an edge. "Did you say *her*?"

"Yes, her name is—"

"Gabrielle," LD finished. "White-blonde, leather outfit, extra dose of crazy in the eyes?"

"You know her?" I asked. "Can you stop her?"

"You tell him, I'll get the bag," LD answered and gestured. Gray runes flew from his hand and hit one of the smooth marble walls. An archway materialized and LD left the Hall of Ten at a run.

"Necromancers are rare in magical circles. Even worse, since they deal with the dead they are usually shunned or thought less capable."

"She seems very capable now," I said. "She froze

Monty in place, and had a mostly dead mage with her under her control."

"She had a very good teacher."

"Who?" I asked. "Is there a dead division of mages that teaches necromancers?"

"William Montague," TK said. "He taught her how to control and increase her ability."

"William? Monty's brother? The same one who taught the Pavormancer that can't be named?"

TK narrowed her eyes at me. "How do you know about Niall?"

"We can say his name?"

"Yes. Fordey isn't on any plane. At least none he can sense," TK replied. "How did you learn his name?"

"Monty and Erik at the Hellfire referred to him without saying his name," I answered, as a portal opened next to us and LD stepped into the Hall. "Why would the Golden Circle appoint William to teach them both?"

"Appoint?" TK said. "The Circle didn't *appoint* him. William kidnapped Gabrielle and lured Niall to him. He kept Gabrielle hostage, and forced Niall to use his ability against his will."

"That's not what Erik and Monty were—"

"They were fed a lie," LD said. "Everyone was. It was to preserve the reputation of the Golden Circle."

"How did they stop Niall?" I asked. "*Were* they able to stop him?"

"The Golden Circle was caught off guard," TK said. "Dex called the Ten and we stopped Niall, but William and Gabrielle escaped."

"Shit, Pavormancers are bad news," LD said, forming

a circle. "She must have freed him."

"From Sheol?" TK asked. "I find that improbable."

"Wait, Sheol as in home for the dead?" I asked, incredulous. "Are there really spirits trapped down there?"

They both looked at me.

LD shook his head. "You have to stop believing in all these fairytales, Simon," he said. "Sheol is like a supermax prison for powerful beings, yes. It's not in the depths of anything, even though it's underground."

"Parts of Sheol are lethal to magic-users. There is an entire area, the null wing, designed by Negomancers," TK said. "Magic is nullified, making executions…"

"…Easy," LD finished. "The danger is that prolonged exposure to the null wing can kill most mages. There are only a few magical classes unaffected by the null wing. One of them is Necromancy. Must be that whole 'death thing' they have going on. Before you ask, no, no spirits are being held there."

"At least to our knowledge." TK grabbed the bag. "Adjust for the oblivion defenses. Erik is a bit on the paranoid side."

"Oh, right," LD said, and gestured again, looking at me. "You coming with us, or are you taking the hellhound express again?"

"Speaking of,"—TK looked down at Peaches, who looked away—"if your hellhound crashes through my defenses again, I will not be making any more sausages."

Peaches whined and nudged my leg, nearly dislocating my hip.

<Tell her it was your fault. You wanted to go to her house.>

<Oh, now it's my fault?>

<She said no more sausages. This is serious.>

<So you understand her?>

<Did you hear what she said? No more sausages. Tell her you're sorry. You won't do it again.>

<What do you mean, I'm sorry? I don't teleport through planes.>

<Meat is life. Say sorry…please.>

I sighed. "It wasn't his fault," I said. "I was the one who had him crash Fordey."

Another deep whine emanated from his cavernous chest. He shook his massive head and put it down on the ground, giving TK his best puppy-dog eyes.

"I see," TK said, while still looking down at Peaches. "In that case I will teach Simon how to make your favorite sausage *after* we help Tristan."

He chuffed, stepping into the circle LD had created.

"I didn't see Erik or the Harlequin," I said, stepping into the circle too. "I don't know what she did to them."

"Let's go find out," LD said, and then gestured.

Fordey Boutique disappeared in a gray cloud.

TEN

ERIK'S OFFICE LOOKED like a book bomb had gone off. Pages were everywhere. Yat lay on top of Erik's desk, bloody and bruised. A cold wave came over me as I looked around, but I didn't see Monty.

"Yat," I said slowly, trying to contain the rage and fear that was crawling up my back. "Where's Monty?"

"Gabrielle took him," he managed through swollen lips. "I know where he is. She will not release him until I give her the location of the White Heart."

My words to Roxanne rushed back: *We'll keep him safe.*

I took a few calming breaths and stopped after I realized it was futile. Monty's absence wasn't having a calming effect, no matter how many breaths I took.

"Where?" I asked. "Where did she take him?"

"You cannot go, Simon," Yat said, turning his face so he could see me with the eye that wasn't swollen shut. "She will kill you."

"Kill me? What do you mean *kill* me?"

"She's gone somewhere that's too dangerous, even for you," he said through cracked lips. "Too dangerous for any of us."

I stepped close. "Show TK where it is," I said, my voice full of tightly controlled frustration. "We'll take you to Haven and then go get Monty."

"Your emotion is clouding your vision," Yat said. "He is not a child."

"He's defenseless," I replied. "He can't cast, and I promised Roxanne I'd keep him safe."

"You should not make impossible promises," Yat said quietly. "You should know better."

"How did he survive the obsidian dust after prolonged exposure?" TK asked. "It should have incapacitated him at Haven."

"He's wearing a bloody bloom," I said. "Maybe that stopped the effect of the dust?"

"How did Tristan get a bloody bloom?" LD looked at TK. "That would do it, though. Bloody blooms are difficult to get."

"Roxanne gave it to him. I just thought it was fancy jewelry with some protective properties. You're saying it's stronger?"

"If Tristan is alive," TK said, "it's because of that bloom."

"So he *is* defenseless," I said, looking at Yat.

"A mage is not his magic, any more than you are merely your gun or blade," Yat said, shaking his head. "He may not be able to cast, but he is far from defenseless."

"I have to go get him. Where did she go?"

Yat shook his head. "No. I will not be responsible for your death. It's too dangerous for you in this state of mind."

"But she *took* Monty," I said. "Do you understand what has happened here?"

"Evidently," he said. "You must ask *why*, Simon. She doesn't need him to achieve her goal; why burden herself with Tristan?"

"Leverage?" I asked, thinking aloud. "But against whom?"

"You are the detective…detect," Yat said, resting his head back against the desk. "I am going to take a moment to enjoy this pain."

"Enjoy the pain?" I looked down at him. "It doesn't look pleasant."

He nodded slowly. "Pain allows me to reflect on the moments when I have none, which are few and far between. It allows me to enjoy my life."

I examined the multitude of bruises and cuts on his body. "Life must be a festival right about now, then. How did she manage to take Monty? You couldn't stop her?"

I turned as I heard footsteps behind me and saw a disheveled Erik in the doorway.

"Stop her?" Erik said as he limped into the office. "By all rights, he should be dead. She attacked and took Tristan after you disappeared with your hound."

"His name is Peaches," I said, more abruptly than I intended. "Where were you?"

"Giving last rites to some of my Harlequin," Erik answered, his voice hard. "And you?"

"Getting help," I said, looking over at TK and LD, who had stepped close to Yat, placing the bag on the floor. "I didn't think Zombie Queen Gabrielle would take Monty."

"None of us did," Erik answered. "She took most of us by surprise."

I looked away and took a deep breath. It made no sense to piss everyone off and act like an ass. I needed help and right now, they were the only ones who could help me find Monty.

"I'm sorry," I said. "I didn't mean to question your location. That didn't come out right. It's just that—"

"We're all concerned, but this is Tristan. Gabrielle may regret taking him. He's not William, and he's not exactly what I would call a soft target."

"Do you know where she took him?" I looked at Yat. "He doesn't want to share."

Erik glanced at Master Yat briefly. "She's gone to the Pit."

Yat gave him a one-eyed glare. If he had access to his staff, I'm certain Erik would've been thwacked a few times.

"Simon, you must not follow her," Yat said, still glaring at Erik. "The Pit is too dangerous."

"He's right, of course, not that you'll listen." Erik nodded to LD and TK. "Can you stabilize him before we move him?"

TK nodded. "We need to do a runic triage. Pass me the runic scanner, dear." LD bent down and rummaged through the bag. He brought out a thin piece of rectangular metal and handed it to TK.

Erik waved a hand and the books began to reassemble. The individual pages floated back into their respective books. Once assembled, the books floated back to their shelves.

"I swear," he said, looking at me. "It's like you and

Tristan are a confluence of chaos. Everywhere you go, destruction follows you. Nothing remains intact for long."

"It's a gift," I said, watching TK work on Yat. "How is he?"

The air of menace behind me made the hairs on the back of my neck stand on end. Several Harlequin appeared at the door and walked into the office. All of their tonfas gave off a deep blue glow.

They fanned out around us, taking strategic positions to fend off another attack. The unspoken threat was palpable in the air. I counted ten, and they looked ready to inflict some tonfa pain.

"They seem angry," I said to Erik, who stood on the other side of the desk. "You don't usually have this many around you at once."

"Harlequin don't like being attacked, or losing one of their own," Erik answered, as he glanced at the Harlequin around the office. "They aren't angry. Right now, they're lethal. Do not provoke them."

I nodded and refocused on TK and LD. Occasionally, I knew when silence was the best response.

LD knelt beside Yat and gestured. TK joined him and traced runes over Yat's body.

"He's suffered internal damage," TK said. "If we try to treat him here, we'll make matters worse. He needs a proper facility."

She looked over at LD, who nodded. "It's not just physical damage." He gestured over Yat's body. "Gabrielle interlaced some nasty failsafes into his energy signature."

"It's clear, but too entangled," TK said, narrowing

her eyes and looking at where LD pointed. "We can't unravel that without causing a fatal cascade."

"Probably didn't have time to hide it," LD said. "Something like this would usually be under several layers of illusion to get a medic to start. Before you know it, whoosh, too late and you lose the patient. Very nasty."

TK nodded. "I'd prefer to leave it to someone who can handle negating these runic phages." TK removed the runic scanner, placing the metal rectangle in the bag again. "As accomplished as LD is, this is beyond us."

"Immediate or delayed?" LD asked, looking at TK. "His vitals are solid and he's responsive."

"He's responsive and his physical status is stable, but those necrophages place him in immediate status." TK looked at Erik. "Tell Haven they'll need a Negomancer to deal with the failsafes first."

Erik made some gestures in the air. "I'll notify Haven. I also have to notify the Council. Yat, did you give her the location?"

Yat gently shook his head. "No, this may be why she took Tristan. To provoke a response or to fend off an attack."

"Where is this Pit?" I asked. "Why can't we go get Monty now?"

Yat nodded at TK. "He is more obstinate than Tristan," Yat said with a sigh. "Tell him. He needs to know why this is foolish."

TK glanced at me. "Do you recall when we discussed the null wing in Sheol?"

I nodded. "Yes, the place that's lethal to most magic-users," I said. "Is that where she is?"

"The Pit is the deepest part of the null wing." TK looked at Yat and continued. "It's a one-way trip to the lowest level in the null wing. No one in the history of Sheol has escaped the Pit...alive."

"Simon, without your curse..." LD said. "If you're caught, there's no coming back."

I understood what they were trying to say. My curse was magical in nature. If the null wing negated magic, it meant I wouldn't be immortal. I could actually *die* in Sheol.

"I get it. There's no magic. It's bullets and blades, then." Peaches rumbled next to me. "Sorry. Bullets, blades, and teeth."

Peaches chuffed and rumbled again.

LD looked at me, shook his head, and smiled. "*You* are insane," he said. "I wish we could go with you."

"Me too. How long before the null wing is lethal to Monty?" I asked. "How long before he loses the protection from the bloom?"

"That would depend on the potency of the bloom," TK replied. "If it's a powerful one, it could withstand the effects of Sheol anywhere from a few hours to several days."

Knowing how Roxanne felt about Monty, she would get the industrial strength bloom to give him. Then a thought occurred.

"Couldn't we just get all of you blooms and storm the castle?" I asked. "If you all wore a bloom, you'd be protected."

"Remember when I said bloody blooms are difficult to get?" LD asked.

I nodded. "We can just get Roxanne to get some

more and—"

"I don't think I was being clear," LD continued. "Whoever creates a bloom has to infuse it with their life energy. They have to be powerful enough to create it, and strong enough to exist without a part of their life energy. It works best if there is some kind of attachment or bond."

"Roxanne is that strong?" I asked. "That would explain Monty's reluctance when she gave it to him."

"For Tristan," TK said, looking at LD, "she probably is, but she can't make blooms for all of us. It would kill her."

"This is a futile exercise," Erik said. "You can't get into the Pit. No one knows where Sheol is, exactly."

"What do you *mean* no one knows?" I turned to Erik. "How can no one know?"

"It's a magical supermax prison," Erik explained. "Designed to keep mages and the like *in*. If everyone knew where it was they would try to break them *out*."

"It operates on the same principle as Fordey," TK said. "It shifts planes constantly. I don't know where it is, but I know someone who does."

"Who?"

"He won't meet us here." She looked around Erik's newly organized office. "We need someplace neutral."

"The Rump?"

She shook her head. "No, still too much ambient magic."

"Peck Slip," I said, looking at Erik. "You said that part of downtown has become a neutral zone."

Erik nodded. "Yes. An entire block is now a magical null zone. Perhaps this mystery person will meet you there."

"I'll pick him up," LD said. "Unless you'd like to, darling?"

"No thanks, dear," TK answered. "He's quite unsettling. Besides, I can utilize the time to help Simon prepare for his trip. I'll meet you on location."

LD gestured and opened a portal. "Give me an hour. He can be hard to find most days."

TK nodded as LD disappeared. She looked over at Erik and then to Yat. "Get him to Haven immediately. Inform Roxanne that Gabrielle attached necrophages to his energy signature. A Negomancer must address those first. Any other treatment risks activating them and ending his life."

"Gabrielle is a nasty piece of work," Erik said, shaking his head. "Hit us all with a walking dead cast. Took out one of my Harlequin without a hindrance and summoned undead."

"Her strength is formidable. I'm sure William helped with that."

"By the time I counterattacked, it was too late," Erik replied. "Animated magical corpses overran us. She can only summon a handful of dead mages, but she can control an army of mindless undead."

"And we happen to be close to the African Burial Ground," I said. "She had all the corpses she needed."

A Harlequin entered the office and whispered into Erik's ear. "Excuse me, we are still recovering from the attack," he said. "I need to address this situation." He turned to speak to the Harlequin.

"I understand," I said, and noticed Yat motioning for me to get closer. I stepped to the desk, where he grabbed my hand and pulled me close. His grip was just this side of bone crushing.

"Do you understand the task you are undertaking?" he said quietly, pulling me even closer.

"I understand I need the bones in my hand intact if I'm going to help Monty," I answered, but he didn't release his vise-like grip. "Are you *trying* to break my hand?"

"Humor is your defense and excellent for deflection," he said. "You use it well, when it isn't earning you correction."

"*Correction*," I said. "Is that what you call all those staff whacks?"

"Did they correct your behavior?"

"Not really."

"I will make sure to redouble my efforts in the future," he replied with a small smile at my expression, and then grew serious. "You must be certain about this, Simon. Are you certain?"

I nodded. "Monty's in danger. You saw him, he's not thinking straight. Now this Gabrielle has him frozen. He needs help."

"You will not have your curse." Yat stared into my eyes. "You will be mortal."

I remained silent for a few seconds and returned the stare. "I know. Doesn't matter. Monty isn't just a friend, he's my family, and he'd do the same for me. No matter where I was."

Yat nodded and closed his eyes for a moment. "Many times, we must choose our family," Yat answered. "Blood determines relation, but choice determines family. Remember that."

"I will."

"If you insist on facing her, you will need this," he said, and suddenly my hand felt like it was on fire. "Perhaps this was my purpose in all of this. Bring back Tristan, before it's too late."

He leaned his head back, closing his eyes again. I looked down at the palm of my hand and saw a series of runes I didn't understand flashing rapidly in sequence. TK leaned over and looked.

"Can you read it?" she asked me. "Do you understand what it says?"

"No, it's just a bunch of flashing runes."

"Look at it again and focus."

I narrowed my eyes and took a deep breath. The runes slowed down long enough for me to see their shapes.

"I can see them." I looked at Yat, but he was unconscious. "What's this?"

"That"—she pointed at my hand—"is the location to Shamballa and the White Heart. Close your hand."

ELEVEN

I CLOSED MY hand. It was still warm from Yat passing me the runes to Shamballa.

"What do you mean, Shamballa?" I asked in a low voice. "You mean it's real?"

"Yes, it's real. As real as any other place."

"Why would he give it to me?" I asked as TK gestured and runes floated from her fingers, leaving green trails in the air. "He should've given it to you."

She shook her head. "LD and I are creative mages. We step into Sheol—or worse, the Pit—and we won't leave alive. You need to do both."

"I'm not a mage."

"That's precisely why he gave it to you," TK said. "We can discuss this later."

Erik turned to us as the Harlequin who had entered earlier left silently. I closed my hand reflexively as he approached.

"You need to go to Peck Slip," he said. "I have revenants roaming the streets of my city and the NYTF is in over their heads, as usual."

"Can you contact Aria?" I asked. "This is important."

"You suddenly need a book from the Wordweavers?" Erik asked. "Do you think it can wait?"

I was tempted, really, but the ten Harlequin around us with glowing tonfa reminded me that Erik was their leader. Insulting him would probably constitute an attack. One they would feel forced to defend against, considering recent events. I didn't want to give them an excuse.

I took a breath, bit my tongue, and measured my words.

"Aria had Yat working on some lost-rune project," I said. "It would be good for her to know what happened to him and where he is."

"Lost-rune project?" Erik asked. "Did she elaborate on which runes she had him searching for?"

"Not really," I said, suddenly cautious. Something about his tone set me off. "Monty wasn't happy about it."

"I'm sure he wasn't," Erik said, tapping his chin. "Lost runes are dangerous. Most are lost for a reason."

"Understood. Can you make sure she knows about Yat and when he arrives at Haven?"

"Of course," Erik said. "Anything else? Would you like me to pack you a lunch?"

"Wait, the Dark Goat. I left it parked outside the entrance to Hellfire."

"I'll have SuNaTran deliver it to you," Erik said. "No one in their right mind would attempt to drive that thing. What is Cecil thinking?"

"I think he's trying to see how destructive we really are, or trying to kill us for London," I said. "Haven't quite figured out which yet."

Erik shook his head. "The runes on that thing—"

"Ramirez isn't going to be able to deal with Zombie Queen and her army," I said, changing the subject. "He's going to lose his mind. This may be a bit beyond the NYTF."

"He's trained not to," Erik said, grabbing a phone. "I'll bring in the Council Mages and deal with things on this end. You go get Tristan back and try to avoid the Pavormancer if you can."

TK brought her hand down and opened a portal. I saw the South Street Seaport through the tear in space she had created. "Take care of Yat," she said. "We'll be back when we can."

We stepped through and I felt a sudden rush, like a huge shove. When I looked around, I saw the portal behind us showing me part of Erik's office.

"No hurry, really," Erik said, swiping his arm and closing the portal.

"You'd think he wasn't happy to have us visit," I said as I looked around.

"You and Tristan have a singular effect on people— mostly aversion."

"He sounded off about the lost runes."

"Mages don't like to speak about the lost runes," TK said. "Most of the runes were lost during the last war. It's a sensitive subject."

We stood in the center of Peck Slip. It wasn't that long ago that we had faced a dragon, a Kragzimik, on this same street. Cobblestones beneath us reminded me of a long forgotten time when these streets were actually busy with ships offloading goods.

Now, Peck Slip was two blocks of empty real estate that had been converted to a plaza type of space, with planters, large stones, and rentable bicycles for the environmentally concerned city dweller. On either side of Peck Slip, developers had transformed the old shipping buildings into upscale lofts and condominiums, making the area a prime location for those working in the financial district.

TK closed her eyes and turned in a small circle. With a nod, she confirmed what I already knew.

"This place isn't just a magical null zone. It's magically dead." She looked at me and raised an eyebrow. "What did you do?"

"*I* didn't do anything," I said, shoving Peaches away from my leg. "This was all Monty, Dex, George, Kristman Dos, and his pack of were-tigers."

"I'm certain you had a part to play in all the mayhem." She looked around and found a bench. "I hardly think you sat this one out."

"I was busy trying to keep this bus of a hellhound from getting us all killed," I muttered, moving Peaches all of six inches. "And trying not to get dragonstomped."

"Of course you were," she said. "We have some time before LD arrives. Are you ready?"

"For what?" I said warily. I'd learned that anytime a mage asks you if you're ready, something is about to explode. It could be an object near you or it could *be* you. Chances were pretty even for either scenario. "Why do I need to be ready?"

"*You* are going to make *your* hellhound his sausage."

I shook my head. "*That* is a bad idea. Besides, we're

in a magical null zone."

"Look at your hand," she said and leaned back. "What's happening?"

The runes Yat had burned into my palm were still flashing in sequence. "How is that possible?" I asked, confused.

"If I had to guess, I'd say it has something to do with your bonds," she said with a shrug. "You'd be better off asking Prof. Ziller. I'm sure he'd enjoy this paradox."

"Pass." I examined the runes on my hand closely. "Speaking to him is like speaking to Monty squared. My brain couldn't handle the magespeak."

"And yet you survived the Sanctuary and meeting Ziller in person. It seems your brain is more resilient than you think."

"Ziller—the books Monty got from Aria, we—?"

"…Have them here." She moved her hand over one side of her body and a satchel materialized. She opened the outer flap and I could see the books Aria gave Monty. I noticed the circular dragonfly insignia in the center of the bag.

"What's that symbol?" I said, pointing to the dragonfly inside of a circle of reeds.

She narrowed her eyes at me. "What do you see?"

"A dragonfly inside a circle of reeds," I said, confused. "What am I supposed to see?"

"Nothing," she said, reaching in the satchel and removing the books. "We may need to have a conversation about your growing abilities."

"How did you…?" I looked at the books she handed me.

"Yat made sure I had them," she said and leaned

forward. "Now, stop stalling. I'm sure your hellhound is hungry."

"The real question is when isn't he hungry?"

<When I'm asleep.>

She rubbed Peaches' head. "When he's asleep would probably be the only time," she said with a nod. "For a hellhound, meat is life and life is meat. Let's get started."

<She is a Zen Meat Guru. You could learn from her.>

<A what?>

<Are you sure she isn't part hellhound?>

<I'm sure. She's going to show me how to make you meat.>

< I trust her. You, not so much. Is this going to be like your magic ball?>

<Magic missile.>

<It didn't taste so good, your magic missile.>

<You aren't supposed to eat it.>

<What is it for, then?>

<To blast through, well, anything.>

<I think you need more magic in your magic missile.>

<I'm not a mage, you know.>

<But you want to handle a magic missile? Maybe we should let her make the sausage?>

<It's going to be the best sausage you've ever had.>

<I think you should practice your magic missile and leave the meat to scary lady.>

"Simon? Are you ready?"

"Sorry, yes, I'm ready…I think."

Peaches whined and turned his head.

"What's wrong with your hellhound?"

"He doesn't exactly think I can do this."

"He's probably right," she said with a smile at

Peaches. "But we're going to give it a try and see what happens."

Peaches chuffed and sat on his haunches.

"The confidence from you two is overwhelming."

"Do you remember the runes?" she asked. "The ones I showed you?"

I thought back to the sequence of runes she had shown me.

"I think so," I said hesitantly. I started tracing the sequence. "Is that it?"

She nodded. "You have to infuse it with energy or it will taste horrible and your hellhound may bite *you*. Try it again."

I traced the sequence again. It flowed easier this time.

"Good. A few more times and then, when you're ready, direct energy into the runes with intention," she said quietly. "Allow the energy to flow."

"What is the intention?" I asked, tracing the runes again.

She narrowed her eyes at me and, for a moment, I thought she was going to blast me. "The *intention* is to make a sausage."

"Right." I nodded. "Just making sure."

She looked down at Peaches, who whined again. "You may be right," she said. "This may be a mistake."

I ran through the sequence again a few times until I felt comfortable and took a deep breath.

"There are no command words? Nothing I need to say?"

TK crossed her arms and leaned back against the bench. "What? Something Latin-sounding and powerful?"

I nodded. "Just wondered," I said. "I'm creating this out of nothing."

"No. You aren't," she corrected. "You are transforming energy from one state to another. Not creating out of nothing. No one is that powerful."

"So no command words?" I asked. "Really?"

"Sure, maybe try *Expecto Sausageum,* that should coax it along," she said with a straight face. "If that doesn't work, try *Windmarium Meatiosa,* should definitely help."

She stared at me, making a waving motion for me to proceed. I stared back. I was new to the world of magic and the supernatural—just not *that* new.

She held it together for another five seconds before breaking into a short laugh. "Sorry. I apologize for laughing at your expense," she said. "I wanted to see what would happen if you did try to create an *Expecto Sausageum.*"

"I'm going to guess nothing?"

"Simon, you aren't a mage."

"I understand that," I answered. "Monty reminds me of it almost daily."

Mentioning Monty brought a rush of urgency and frustration to my thoughts.

"No, you misunderstand." She held up a hand. "You're not a mage or a wizard or anything else I've come across. You're a unique blend of a cursed human with latent magical ability. Which is no longer latent. You're also bonded to a hellhound, a siphoning Seraph blade, and have some strange connection to a personification of Karma."

"So I'm some kind of…mutant?" I said with a smile. "Like Wolverine?"

She glared at me. "I don't know *what* you are," she answered. "Besides one half of a mobile demolition crew."

"Most of that is Mage Montague and my trusty hellhound," I said, looking down at Peaches, who was lying down and looking away. "You said it, I'm not a mage."

"That may be true, but you are a nexus for destruction," she replied, shaking her head. "You may not be causing it, but you're never far from it. It's almost as if chaos follows you."

Her words chilled me as I remembered the old god who tried to destroy us.

"Fine, I'll concede that point," I said with a shudder. "Maybe the company I keep is a little on the explosive side. That doesn't help me with this sausage thing or my magic missile."

"All it means is that you *specifically* can't adhere to the usual way of doing things." She gestured and formed a sausage, giving it to the perpetually hungry Peaches, who inhaled it instantly. "The way we do things will not always be the way you do things. Figure it out."

"So no command words?"

She materialized a green orb of angry-looking energy in one hand. "Make your hellhound a sausage, emphasis on *edible*."

"An orb of angry death isn't helping, you know."

"Now."

I focused, closed my eyes, and traced the runes she had taught me. I concentrated on a sausage that would be tasty *and* healthy for Peaches, he *was* putting on some pounds. I finished the runes and willed energy into the action.

On the ground in front of Peaches was a large sausage. TK nodded her approval and absorbed the green orb of pain.

"Not bad," she said and patted Peaches. "Now we have to see if he will eat it."

<Is it safe?>

<Of course it's safe. I made it.>

<That's why I'm asking. You made it.>

<You didn't even stop to think before you ate her sausage.>

<She makes delicious meat. You make disgusting magic balls.>

<Missiles. Magic missiles.>

<Not really. Are missiles supposed to roll at their targets?>

<Nevermind that. You're always asking me to make you meat. There you go.>

He lowered his nose to the sausage and sniffed, quickly pulling his face away.

<It smells different. Why does it smell like leaves?>

<I added broccoli since you're getting heavy. Figured I'd make you a healthy sausage.>

<Heavy? I'm a hellhound. I'm supposed to be heavy.>

<You almost snapped the elevator cable in Haven. You're not supposed to be that heavy.>

<A healthy sausage? Is it meat?>

<Yes, it's meat. Meat is life. Go on. Eat it.>

He grabbed one end and took a nibble.

<That's good. It could use more meat.>

<It's a meat sausage. How could it use more meat?>

<Remove the leaves.>

<This is so you could eat sausage and be healthy. It's good for you.>

<I'm a little hungry so I'll eat this one. The next one you make needs more meat.>

As he ate the sausage, I heard a truck coming down the street. It was a SuNaTran flatbed transporting the Dark Goat.

"Seems like it's edible," TK said. "What are those green flakes?"

Peaches finished off the sausage and rolled on his side.

"See, it was so good it sent him into a food coma," I said. "Maybe we could start the 'Montague and Strong Detective Agency and Butcher Shop'?"

"Simon, the green flakes your hellhound just consumed. What were they?"

"Broccoli," I said proudly. "If he's going to eat this much sausage, he may as well have some veggies to go with it. Don't you think? Nice balanced diet with plenty of greens."

Her eyes widened slightly in surprise. "Are you serious?"

"Of course. Look how heavy he's getting."

We both looked down at the prone Peaches. He gave me a look and flopped his head to the other side.

"He's a hellhound, being heavy comes with the breed," she said, shaking her head. "You've given a hellhound a sausage laced with broccoli."

I nodded. "I used intention like you suggested and created the Healthy Hellhound Delight," I answered. "Not bad for my first try. What do you think?"

"What do I *think*?" she said, getting up. "Your first try may end up being your last."

"What are you talking about?" I pointed at Peaches.

"He loved it. Look at him, he can barely move."

"You have no idea, do you?" TK said, shaking her head. "You've just created deathane. Giving broccoli to a hellhound? Are you insane?"

A portal formed across the street as I was about to answer. I felt a tremor and saw TK move suddenly across the street. Peaches remained where he was, then chuffed and growled.

<My body doesn't feel so good.>

<You probably have to get used to the new, healthier diet.>

<Your meat is making me feel full of air.>

<Full of air? What do you mean full of air?>

<Your meat is not life. Your meat is unlife.>

I crouched down to rub his belly. TK's words rushed back. *You've just created deathane.*

I froze and turned to run across the street, but it was too late. Peaches stood and introduced me to ground-zero hellhound gas.

TWELVE

I HEARD IT before I smelled it.

The sound of a jackhammer originated deep in his belly. When it finally arrived, it was the sound of machine gun fire under heavy artillery. The sound surprised me, but nothing could prepare me for the stench.

As the cloud of broccoli-induced hellhound deathane engulfed and strangled me, I realized that even with immortality, this was an odor that could end me. My eyes started tearing up. The sensation of heat was so strong, I looked down to make sure my skin wasn't melting off my bones.

Every part of me that was exposed burned and the miasma that had been transparent only a moment earlier had become a dark gray with red overtones. Everywhere I could see, I only saw darkness. I took short shallow breaths, with each exhalation setting my throat on fire.

<What are you doing, boy? Is this a new weapon?>
<Your meat of unlife doesn't feel good at all.>

<I'm sorry. I think I need more practice.>

<Next time you eat a sausage first.>

I heard another rumble begin in his stomach.

<Boy, that doesn't sound good.>

<Because it isn't. Get away while you still can.>

I wrapped my arms around his neck.

<I'm staying right here. Can you not blow us up into little bits though?>

<I have no control over this.>

The noise that accompanied the next expulsion of gas was epic in volume and force. It launched us across the street and into the wall next to the portal that had just formed.

I bounced off the wall and rolled into the street. A warm flush filled my body as it dealt with the damage of cannonballing into a building. Peaches slammed into the wall, shattering some of the brick, and dropped to the ground. He padded over next to me, shook his entire body, and slobbered all over my face.

<My saliva will help you. Too bad yours can't help me after your meat of unlife.>

LD came into my field of vision. "Are you practicing a new evasion tactic with your hellhound? Crash and smash?"

It took a few minutes for the street to stop seesawing once I sat up. TK stepped close to me and let some golden runes fall across my head. I immediately felt better.

"That should help," she said, scrunching up her nose. "I should let you reap what you've sown, but I enjoy having my lungs intact. That stench is probably fatal."

With a swipe of her arm, a light breeze blew the rest

of the smell away, replacing it with the smell of cinnamon. My stomach clenched and I looked around, making sure Karma wasn't making an appearance.

I gently pushed Peaches back to stop the slobber bath and noticed she'd managed to cast in a magical dead zone.

<Thank you, but I'm good.>

<Your sausage is not good.>

<Maybe no broccoli next time. Explosive sausage is too dangerous.>

<Any sausage you make is too dangerous.>

<Not true, this was my first try. Next time I'll focus more. We can try low-fat sausage.

<Next time?>

"Is that him?" I heard a voice say. "Does he usually enjoy flying into walls? I can guarantee you that won't work in Sheol."

LD looked at TK and raised an eyebrow.

"He created his first sausage," TK said with a nod. "Which the hellhound found edible."

"What did he do, lace it with C4?" LD asked with a smile. "Why the aerial maneuvers, then?"

"Broccoli." TK gestured and created another sausage for my bottomless pit of a hellhound. "He felt the sausage should be *healthy*."

LD crouched down so that our eyes were level. He shook his head slowly. "Don't ever feed your hellhound broccoli. You'll just create—"

"…Deathane," I said, rubbing my head and shakily getting to my feet. "Got it."

LD nodded and clapped me on the shoulder. "Congrats on the first sausage, even if it resulted in percussive gluteal impacts," he said with a laugh. "Hombre, you got your ass kicked by a sausage!"

The man next to him chuckled and even TK smiled slightly.

"You're never going to let me forget this, are you?"

"Of course, in a thousand years, maybe," LD said with another laugh. "Hey, your nightmaremobile is here."

The flatbed holding the Dark Goat parked and I saw Robert get out. He pulled some levers and the rear of the truck angled upward. Once the Dark Goat was off the flatbed, he approached holding a clipboard.

"Good afternoon, sir," Robert said, handing me the clipboard. "If you'd be so kind to sign off on the delivery of your…vehicle?"

I had never seen Robert appear nervous. It was clear the Dark Goat unsettled people. It unsettled me, and I was its driver.

"Are you okay, Robert?" I held the pen over the clipboard. "You seem a little out of sorts."

"I'm fine, sir." He pointed at the clipboard. I could see the sweat on his face. "Signature, please?"

"Did anyone try and drive the car?" I asked.

"No, sir," Robert answered. "We have clear instructions regarding this specific vehicle."

"Good," I said. "Don't want Cecil holding me responsible for one of his drivers getting erased."

"We'll be careful, sir," Robert replied. "I am a little pressed for time, if you don't mind."

I signed the release form and handed him the clipboard. "Thank you, Robert. Let Cecil know I'm still alive and his Goatabomination is still intact."

"Will do, sir." He tipped his cap and nearly sprinted back. He turned before getting into the truck. "Good day, sir."

I waved as he pulled away and sped off, leaving the Dark Goat on the street. I could see the smoke wafting up from its surface as the color fluctuated from deep purple to black.

"He seemed nervous," I said, turning to LD, TK and the mystery man. "Who's this?"

"This is the person who's going to take you to Sheol." LD pointed at the man next to him. "Mark Ronin, meet Simon Strong. Half of the infamous Montague and Strong Demolition Agency."

THIRTEEN

I EXTENDED A hand and we shook. He was tall and wore a dark suit, dark shirt, and dark shoes.

"Funeral casual? Is that the go-to for magic types?"

"Easier to hide blood splatter," TK said, looking me over. "You may want to upgrade your wardrobe as well. Dragonscale is a useful passive deterrent from Tristan's spell casting and your hellhound adventures."

"What hellhound adventures?"

She raised an eyebrow at me and looked at the wall I had just smashed into minutes earlier.

"The ones that usually end up with buildings collapsing."

"That was an accident," I said, pointing at the cracked brick. "Lots of these buildings down here are really old."

"You and Tristan seem to have a surplus of accidents," she said. "Have Piero make you some dragonscale suits."

I glanced over at Mark. The 'man in black trainees' suit looked like an Armani with custom alterations. If I had to guess I'd say it was lined with dragonscale.

"Pleasure, Mark," I said. "You know how to get to —?"

"Ronin, Call me Ronin," he said. "Let's get some things straight right away. I'm only here because we owe Dexter and the Ten. LD, I still don't know how you found me."

"You can run, but you can't hide," LD answered, wiggling his fingers and wagging an eyebrow. "At least not from me."

TK nodded. "You'd think he'd learn that by now?"

"Who's 'we'?" I asked, looking at Ronin. "You said *we*. Who do you work for?"

Ronin looked over at LD, who gave him a slight nod.

"I'm Division 13 or at least I was," he said. "My last case put me on an…extended leave."

"They bounced you out of Division 13?"

"Officially, yes," he said with a nod. "Unofficially, no. I needed latitude I didn't have within the Division. That's about as much as I'm going to say about that."

"So you're here under protest?" I looked at LD. "Why is he here if he's not going to help?"

"Hear him out," LD said, raising a hand. "Ronin is good people, even if he thinks he can hide from me."

"I didn't say I wasn't going to help, Simon. We've been watching you and frankly there are a few in the Division that feel Tristan belongs in Sheol and you right next to him. Along with that" —he pointed at Peaches —"large animal you call a pet."

"His name is Peaches and he's not a pet."

"He's also not normal. I just saw him smash into a brick wall at high speed and shake it off."

"He's on a high-protein diet," I said. "He loves meat."

"Right, do you really want to do this?" Ronin asked.

"Do what?"

Ronin touched his forearm. "Cait, bring up the Montague and Strong file. It's listed under mayhem and property damage."

"Who's Cait?" I asked, looking at LD. "Who's he talking to?"

Ronin held up a finger. "Got it. Corneal display, please."

"What are you talking about?" I asked. "LD? Does he need meds or something?"

"Pay attention, Simon." LD pointed at Ronin. "He's about to share."

"Where do I begin? Chaos—the god, not the general state that follows you around—on Roosevelt Island," Ronin started. "Two void vortices *inside* the city, a plague of werewolves resulting in several NYTF fatalities. Blood Hunters—which by the way haven't been seen on this continent in centuries."

"You weren't looking in the right places."

"Oh, we were looking, they just weren't *here*. Then you go to London and decide the Tate Modern needs a destructive makeover along with most of the city. Several bridges had to be repaired or replaced."

"To be fair, London is really old."

"Speaking of old—the Tower of London is still being restored brick by brick because of you and another goddess, the Morrigan."

Ronin rubbed a temple and sighed.

"You don't think we can actually *control* the

Morrigan?" I asked. "Have you met her, she's—"

"…In a class of her own and also has some strange thing going with Dexter. I know."

"Then you know the Tower wasn't really—"

"I'm not done. After trouncing London, and I suggest you avoid Europe for a few decades since Penumbra would like to have you flayed, you head to the Sanctuary."

"How is *that* Division 13 business?"

"If it impacts this plane, it's Division 13 business. Where was I? Oh, the Sanctuary, which is currently under reconstruction after your last visit."

"That was mostly Oliver and his gray band of psychopaths."

"Which we were poised to neutralize until your partner made it personal."

"His father was in danger," I said, my voice hard. "His *father*. You wanted him to ignore that?"

"There are channels and methods. You and your partner follow neither."

"I didn't realize there was a Division 13 hotline. You have a red phone somewhere with a direct line?"

"Gracie Mansion is now good for toothpicks and kindling. Right here where we're standing is the center, not of a null zone but a magical dead zone. Did I miss anything?"

"Plenty, what's your point?" I said, remembering Hybrid, the Foundry, Ellis Island, and a few other assorted destructions. I could feel the anger rising in my chest. "Where was Division 13 when we were facing all of these threats? I must've missed your people when I stood in front of a dragon ready to help me lose weight by flattening me into a bloody smear on this street."

"We were—" Ronin started.

"No. My turn," I said, pointing at his face. "When this city is about to get crushed, it's me and Monty who rush into the danger. While you, the Dark Council, and all the other operatives hide in the shadows, *we're* the ones facing down the monsters."

"That you usually antagonize in the first place."

"Right, like we antagonized Chaos into wanting to destroy everything," I snapped back. "His job description is right there in his name!"

Ronin shook his head. "Our scope is much larger. We need to control what can impact the entire plane if we —"

"Bullshit," I spat. "Don't give me bureaucratic doublespeak. Your Division doesn't like to get their hands dirty. I'm pretty sure that's why you needed *latitude*. So spare me the laundry list. I know what we've done and, more importantly, I'm willing to burn this city to the ground if it means saving Monty. So I just need to know one thing."

"What is that?"

"Are you going to help me break into Sheol or do I do this on my own?"

"You can't find Sheol on your own. It's a trans-dimensional location. It shifts between planes regularly."

"Like Fordey?"

"Even more complicated than Fordey," Ronin answered with a smug look. "But loosely based on the same principles. Sheol moves around."

"If Peaches can find Fordey, I'm sure he can find

Sheol."

"Impossible. No one can track Sheol," Ronin answered. "That's why we have nodes and locations of alignment."

I looked at LD and motioned with my head to Ronin. "Tell him."

Ronin looked at LD. "Tell me what?" he asked. "You know I'm right. Doesn't matter if it's a hellhound. What's he going to do? Sniff out Sheol?"

"Something like that," LD replied, looking down at Peaches. "He'll track Tristan and if he locates him, then —"

"...He locates Sheol," I finished. "So stop wasting my time. If you're going to help, then help; if not, get out of my way."

"You try going in that way and all of Sheol's defenses will be unleashed," Ronin said. "You'll be dead inside five seconds—really dead."

Ronin looked at LD.

"Told you," LD said, shaking his head. "He's serious."

"Of course, I'm serious. Wait, serious about what?"

"You're right," Ronin said, holding up a hand in surrender. His entire demeanor shifted. "Even though Division 13 is keeping tabs on you."

"Keeping tabs?"

"Your partner unleashed two void vortices inside of the city." He stared at me hard, and I relented with a nod. "We needed to know if he was a threat and placed him, *and* you, under constant surveillance."

"Fair enough, but in Monty's defense, there were extenuating circumstances."

"Seems there always are with you two—sorry, three," Ronin said, glancing over at Peaches. "Division 13 rarely acts fast enough to combat immediate threats. Part of it is the leadership. Most of it is the entrenched mindset."

"Division 13 doesn't like to get their hands dirty," I said. "It has the 'let the peons we pee upon deal with those minor threats' mentality. I mean why focus on the *city*, when we save the entire plane?"

This time Ronin looked away. "I'm not proud of the attitude, but yes, it's something I'm trying to change."

"From the outside," I said, connecting the dots. "That's why you're on *extended leave*. Why the 'laundry list of disaster'?"

"I needed to know if you were determined to do this or if this was just bravado," Ronin answered. "I'm not big on suicide missions."

"Is that what this is? A suicide mission?"

"You've never been to Sheol," he said. "Where we're going, even immortals can die."

FOURTEEN

"WE CAN'T EXTRACT Monty yet," I said, looking at TK and then at my palm with the flashing runes. "Now I know why Yat gave this to me."

"What do you mean we can't extract Tristan yet?" LD said. "Time's against us. Tristan doesn't have long."

"We need to go to Shamballa."

"Shamballa?" LD asked. "Gabrielle is in Sheol, not Shamballa. How *hard* did you hit your head?"

TK nodded. "It makes sense, yes," she said. "Convincing them will be…difficult."

"I'm glad it makes sense to someone," LD said, throwing his hands up in the air. "Can one of you explain it to me?"

"Gabrielle doesn't want or need Monty, she wants the White Heart," I said.

"Which we *don't* want to give her." LD stared at TK. "Right?"

"If we give her the White Heart, what is the next target?" I asked. "Where will she go next?"

"She'll give the Heart to Ni—the Pavormancer and

then we are done. He'll amplify his power and smush us like bugs. I'm not in the mood to be smushed, Simon."

"After she gives him the White Heart, what does he need? What is he after?"

"The Gray Heart…Oh, shit," LD said. "We really are going to get smushed. He needs the Black Heart."

"He can't attempt it without the White Heart, Fordey is too well defended, but once he has it, that should be his next move. It's what I would do."

"And your best idea is to give him the White Heart?" LD asked. "Because that sounds like a horrible idea."

"Sure," Ronin said. "This way you control the what and the where, even though you can't control the when."

"We can control the when, but it's going to take some creative destruction," I said.

"That shouldn't be too hard for you," LD said. "You and Tristan are masters of destruction by now."

"We're going to need to move the Black Heart," I answered. "Do you have somewhere safe where it can be moved to when he finds it, a place where it won't kill millions of people?"

"You mean somewhere you and Tristan don't have access to?" LD asked. "Yes" —he glanced at TK—"we have just the place."

"Hilarious, really," I said, turning to Ronin. "Can you show us how to find Sheol?"

"I can't show *you*," Ronin said, "but I can show them. It's a mage thing, sorry."

"This won't work without the White Heart, will it?" I asked. "You have some kind of temporal displacer on you, right?"

He pulled up his sleeve and showed me a hi-tech vambrace, or forearm-guard.

"This is a Combat Artificially Intelligent Techbrace, or CAIT for short," he said. "It has a few uses, but the CAIT series contains a small temporal displacement chip. That allows me to enter Sheol wherever it is."

I narrowed my eyes and tried to get a sense of his energy signature. "You don't read like a mage."

"Never said I was," Ronin answered. "Mages don't wear techbraces. Goes against the whole 'wand thing' they have going on."

"I thought that was just Monty. It's all mages?"

"To some degree. Your partner is just a bit more… vehement in his dislike of wizards. He'd never wear one of these."

"That's not a wand," I said, looking at the brace.

"Far from it, but mages are touchy about needing something other than their knowledge."

"Looks like the op braces the NYTF use."

"The model they use is a simplified version of this, without the neural connectivity."

The sleek matte black techbrace looked like a forearm-guard made of some hi-tech material. I noticed a large display in its center. The NYTF had something similar, but nothing this advanced. This was decades ahead of the techbraces used by Ramirez and his people.

"That has an operational neural net?" I asked, impressed. "They told us in the NYTF the technology wasn't available."

Ronin nodded. "The CAITs do," he said. "but it won't be released for another decade or so."

"How do we mimic that with the White Heart?" I asked as I admired the device. "It's not like we can create a techbrace."

"You don't need to," Ronin said. "The temporal displacement will allow you access to Sheol once you align to its location on this plane."

"How do we access Sheol?"

"Sheol can only be accessed from Randalls Island, which is about an hour from here."

"We can open a portal there," I said. "That's the easy part."

Ronin shook his head. "There are priming runes along the span of the HellGate Bridge, the old railway that connects to Randalls Island," he said. "You don't cross the bridge. You won't access Sheol. It's a failsafe. The bridge is covered with both conventional and magical defenses."

"That means we need to drive over." I looked over at the Dark Goat. "I'm pretty sure we can handle the defenses. Show them what to do when we get to the alignment location."

"I can show you what you need to do," Ronin said, looking down at this brace, "but once we leave this dead zone, I need to go underground. I have some unpleasant individuals sniffing around who would like to ghost me."

FIFTEEN

WE STOOD NEXT to the Dark Goat as Ronin shared some runic sequences with TK and LD. These were runes I'd never seen before and even if I could understand the symbols, he moved his hands too fast for me to follow.

Peaches was sprawled out in the backseat, recovering from my healthy sausage, and milking it for all it was worth. Every few seconds I'd hear a whine followed by a low growl.

<Stop being such a drama hound.>

<You broke my stomach.>

<There's no way to break a stomach, especially not a hellhound one. You'd eat bricks if they were sausage-shaped.>

<Only if they tasted good.>

<I just need more practice and you need to get it together.>

<Were you trying to hurt me?>

<I would never try to hurt you.>

<My stomach disagrees.>

<We're bondmates. I'd never try to hurt you.>

<Don't make any more magic meat.>

"Do you understand the sequence?" Ronin asked LD again. "If you miss it, you're done. You lose your window, which means you're stuck on the bridge with several dozen angry guards incoming."

"Got it," LD said. "Once I complete this sequence, it'll shunt Simon into Sheol and he'll be on his own?"

"It'll teleport him *and* the hellhound if he keeps him in proximity," Ronin answered. "And it should send him right into the Pit and to Tristan if you interlace the tracking rune into the sequence."

"What's the minimal safe distance?" TK asked. "I have no intention of paying Sheol a visit."

"About three feet," Ronin replied. "Any closer and you're taking a permanent tour of Sheol."

"Glad to hear it's a precise calculation," I said.

"Is he always such a smart-ass?" Ronin asked, glancing at me. "Or is it only when he's pissing his panties?"

"Everyone's a comedian today," I answered. "That's the way in. How do I get out once I find Monty?"

"Same way you were planning to locate your partner if I didn't help you," Ronin said. "Or do you and your hellhound only specialize in destroying national monuments of importance?"

"No. Actually, on occasion we'll destroy random items of little relevance," I answered. "Monty and I are equal opportunity agents of mayhem."

"I would've shot him long ago," Ronin said to LD. "Don't know how you do it."

"Small doses," LD answered. "Like poison."

I stared at them. "And I'm the smart-ass?"

"Can you do it?" LD asked, concerned. "Because if

Peaches can't get you out, you and Tristan will be stuck in the Pit…permanently. There's no cavalry coming to get you."

I looked over at my sprawled-out hellhound. "We can do it. Let's go find the White Heart."

"I'll relocate the Black Heart, dear," TK said. "You go with Simon."

"Right, I'm off," Ronin said. "Division 13 is watching you, Simon. Try not to blow up the city. The last thing you want to do is meet Luca face to face."

LD shuddered. "That would be bad," he said. "Is she still cranky?"

"Only when she's awake. I'll try and help if I can, but I currently have my hands full, with some psychotic who thinks all mages should die."

"Sounds serious," I said. "And *that* impacts the whole plane?"

"Dead mages with their hearts ripped out impact *me*," Ronin said. "The group behind these acts impacts the entire plane. If they're killing mages, no one is safe."

I nodded. I didn't pretend to understand what he was talking about. If someone was going around killing mages, it sounded dangerous. It'd been my experience that mages were notoriously difficult to kill. I just wanted to give him a hard time because he came across like a self-important ass.

"Good luck, hope you stop him, or them."

"Thanks, I don't plan on stopping them, I plan on *killing* them," Ronin answered, looking down at the display on his techbrace. "Cait, pull up the location of the last magekiller attack."

Ronin showed the display to LD, who nodded and

gestured. Gray runes floated from his fingers as another portal opened.

Ronin paused before stepping through. "Don't linger in Sheol. If you manage to get the Gray Heart, you need to find a way to make sure no one can access it."

"Or destroy it," I added.

"Something you have some skill at," Ronin said with a nod. "Go save your friend. Try to keep the plane intact."

He stepped through the portal and disappeared as it closed behind him. Again, I marveled at how much power a creative mage must wield if they could use their ability in a magical dead zone.

"Is it me or is he a little full of himself?" I asked, looking at the location of the portal. "And who's Luca?"

"Ronin is solid." LD gestured, making sure the portal was completely sealed. "He's spent a little too much time in the dark. Division 13 is so far down the rabbit hole they lose touch with reality."

"Makes for poor social skills," TK added. "But he's an accomplished technomancer and one of the best in the Division, after Luca."

"Luca is—?"

"Who you meet when it's the end of the world," LD replied. "When it's all falling apart and you don't see a way out, that's who you want watching your back."

"You've worked with her?" I asked. "She sounds dangerous."

TK nodded. "Luca is one of the Ten. Which is all we can or will share."

I nodded. Everyone was entitled to secrets. What

little I knew about the Ten made me glad I never had to face them as enemies.

"Can it be done?" I asked, looking at LD. "Can we destroy the Heart?"

LD shook his head slowly.

"These are solid runes, hombre," he said. "You would need some next-level energy to undo those things. They were created by Archmages who could wield more power with a thought than several mages together."

"That's power I don't have," I muttered, thinking about my magic missile.

"Or will ever have," LD said. "Not even the both of us together"—he pointed at TK—"would try to undo either of the Hearts."

"The repercussions from that would be incalculable." TK shook her head. "Aside from the immediate death of the mage attempting it."

"Could Master Yat do it?"

They looked at each other silently before LD let out a sigh.

"Yat is—" LD started.

"Let me guess," I said, holding up a hand. "He's complicated."

TK nodded. "Yat is very old and he wields magic in some of the most unconventional methods," she said. "No one knows how powerful or weak he really is."

"He can be hurt, though." I thought back to his bruised and battered body after what Gabrielle had done to him.

"He faced a Necromancer with a staff," TK replied. "Even with all of my ability I would be reluctant to face a full-fledged necromancer like Gabrielle."

"The answer to your question is we don't know," LD said. "Master Yat has been a mystery to most of us for as long as we've known him."

Somehow, Aria thought Master Yat possessed the ability to destroy the White Heart if it came down to it. I would need to look into that. First, we needed to get to Shamballa.

Peaches sauntered out of the Dark Goat and sidled up to my leg with a chuff. He was still letting me have it about his near-health encounter with the sausage I'd made.

"Where are you moving the Black Heart?" I asked, ignoring my pouty hellhound. "Or is that confidential?"

"The Fordey Magical Vault," TK said. "If the White Heart is handed over, he will attempt to join the two. We'll wait for him there. One way or another the Hearts won't leave the vault."

"That sounds final," I said, looking at her. "Are you planning on blowing up the vault?"

"If it comes to that...yes," she replied seriously. "The Gray Heart can't leave the vault."

"Are you going to be able to do this solo, darling?" LD asked. "Moving the Black Heart is going to be tricky."

TK gave LD a look and he put up his hands in surrender with a smile.

"I think I can manage," she said in a tone that cautioned violent pain if he questioned her ability further. "Remember the temporal wells in Shamballa. Time flows differently there."

LD nodded. "Let's go get blissed," he said, opening a

portal.

SIXTEEN

WE STEPPED THROUGH the portal and arrived on the side of a snowcapped mountain. I looked down the slope and into the valley below, where I saw a large temple complex surrounded by a wall.

Outside of the temple grounds were homes and open-air plazas. Fountains and decorative sculptures were situated in the center of the plazas. Waterfalls dotted the sides of some of the mountains and I could see stone bridges connecting some of the smaller peaks to each other.

At the top of some of the mountains, I saw more temples and large buildings. The valley was a lush green and the smell of freshly cut grass wafted up the slope and embraced us. Enormous monarch butterflies flitted erratically around the flowers. Birds I'd never seen before were visible in the air and in some of the trees.

Despite being high above the valley, I felt the warmth of the sun on my face. A cool, sweet-smelling breeze blew past us that carried the scent of the ocean.

"Where exactly is this?" I asked, looking around.

LD pointed down the mountain path to the valley. "That is Shamballa or Shangri-la. If you had to get here from our plane, I'd say the best way would be Tibet and then head west to Ngari."

"I didn't think this place was real."

"It's not," LD said, serious. "You must clear your mind of all attachment and allow your consciousness to become one with your surroundings."

"What?" I said, confused. "This is an illusion?"

He burst into laughter and started walking down the mountain. "Of course it's real," he said between chuckles. "But I do an awesome Master Yat. Should've had a staff to whack you. That would've been perfect."

I shook my head, smiled, and followed him down. He'd totally pulled a Yat on me.

"Where do you think they keep the White Heart?"

"I'm sure they don't have tours through the place," LD said. "Why don't we ask the Abbot if they'll be willing to lend it to us?"

"Wait, TK said time flows differently here," I said, grabbing the threads of an idea. "Are they using the White Heart to keep Shamballa hidden?"

LD stopped walking and turned to face me. "How have you managed to stay alive so long?" he asked and then shook his head. "Sorry, forgot your curse. I don't know, but there is a good chance the White Heart has something to do with keeping this place interstitial."

"If that's the case, they aren't just going to give us the White Heart. Not if it endangers this entire place."

"If Niall gets the Gray Heart, you think this is going to remain a paradise for long?"

"I'm going to go with door number two and say no."

LD nodded and stopped walking. Five robed men and women were walking up the mountain path.

"You know how you are usually an annoying and a monumental pain in the ass?"

"No." I glanced at LD. "Why don't you tell me how you really feel?"

"I'm going to need you to be the opposite of whatever it is you think is proper behavior," LD said under his breath. "Or this is going to be a painfully short trip."

"Are these monks dangerous?" I asked. "They look friendly. Some of them are even smiling."

"That's because you haven't destroyed a temple yet."

The monks were dressed in saffron robes, with the three in the center, two women, and one man, wearing a deeper vermillion overlay. All of them had shaved heads. The center male wore a long string of beads around his neck. It looked like a larger version of the mala beads I had around my wrist.

"I didn't know women could be monks?"

"That's because you need to get out more," LD replied. "Of course women can be monks."

"Welcome," the center monk said with a bow. "I am Zhuchi. Please, come with me."

"You honor us with your presence," LD said, returning the bow and gently caressing my kidneys with a fist when I didn't bow. "Thank you for seeing us, Khen Rinpoche."

"The honor is mine, I have a guest here who has been waiting for you," Zhuchi said with a knowing smile. "Someone who needs your help."

"Our help?" LD answered. "How could someone be

waiting for us? We just planned this trip here recently."

"Indeed," Zhuchi said. "The same way the celestial bodies move through the universe. Always where they need to be."

He turned and headed back down the mountain path with the other monks in tow.

I stared at them as they walked away. I must've been in a slight state of shock, because LD had to nudge me to get me to move forward. I didn't think it was possible, but Zhuchi spoke Yat-ese even better than Master Yat.

"Stop staring," LD said under his breath. "They'll think you're being rude."

"Did you just hear him?" I asked, keeping my voice low as we followed the monks. "If he's going to speak like that, we're going to need a translator."

<Do you think they have meat?>

<I don't think monks eat meat, boy. Can you wait?>

<How can anyone not eat meat? Did you make them one of your magic meats too? Is that why they won't eat meat now?>

<No. That's not the reason. I think most monks don't eat meat, but I don't know about the ones from this place. Maybe they eat hellhounds. Should I ask them?>

<I can wait a little longer.>

I held back a smile as we descended down the mountain and headed to the main temple complex.

SEVENTEEN

THE MONKS LEFT us alone once we entered the temple. We stood in a large open meditation hall. The sunlight streamed in from one side of the temple and gently illuminated the wooden floor. A large plain runner dominated the center of the room. On either side of the runner sat small cushions on square mats.

"Have you been here before?" I asked, taking in the stillness of the room. "How is someone waiting for you?"

"I have no idea," LD answered. "It's not my first time, but the last time I was here it was a slightly more violent circumstance."

"Why doesn't that surprise me?"

"They aren't going to just give you the White Heart, you know," a familiar voice carried over to us from the far side of the meditation hall. "You should just go back now."

"We can't do that," LD said, turning slowly. "What the hell are you doing here?"

I turned to look at a tall older man shrouded in the

shadows of the hall. He was dressed in saffron monk robes and his gray hair was short. His features were vaguely familiar. I had a feeling I knew him somehow.

"Do I know you?" I asked, peering into the shadows. His energy signature was diffuse, as if he were all over the place.

"You may know of me," the man said. "I have been known to get around."

It was an odd sensation, like having the right word on the tip of your tongue. He couldn't have been a full-fledged monk with a head full of hair. Maybe a guest?

LD formed gray orbs of energy around his hands and I placed my hand on Grim Whisper. Peaches, sensing the tension, rumbled next to me.

"Why are we drawing on the unarmed monk?"

"I'd suggest against that course of action, LD," the man said. "Trust me. It won't end well—for you."

"You know him?" I glanced at an angry LD. A nimbus of tight fury surrounded him and had just kicked into overdrive. This was going to shift into one of those mage *conversations* I enjoyed so much. "He knows you? Can we speak before we unleash the massive destruction I'll get blamed for?"

LD nodded, absorbed the orbs, and stayed in a defensive position. "He doesn't look familiar to you?"

I nodded as the man stepped forward into the sunlight. For a moment, my world tilted and I shook my head. It was like looking at an older version of Monty. Except this version bore a scar down one side of his face.

"What are you doing here, William?" LD said, lacing his words with barely suppressed anger. "Tell me why I shouldn't reduce you to ash where you stand."

"You can't," William answered matter-of-factly. "Not in here."

"You're strong, but not *that* strong," LD said, and I felt the energy coalesce around his body. "Last time you had help. This time I'm going to end you."

"Are you *still* angry?" William asked. "I told you it wasn't personal. Just business."

"Don't worry, Billy," LD said, his voice hard. "This won't be too personal."

"The name is William, not Billy." William adjusted his robe. "When I said you can't, I wasn't questioning your ability or desire. I was merely stating fact."

"*This* is William Montague?" I asked. "Monty's brother?"

William turned to me as if noticing me for the first time. He looked at me with a sniff and gave me the 'you're just a roach on the bottom of my shoe' expression.

"Does Tristan allow you to call him 'Monty' to his face?"

"Allow me?" I asked, perplexed for a second. "What do you mean *allow* me? We're friends—more than that, we're family."

William closed the distance and looked me up and down. Close up, the resemblance was unmistakable. He even shared some of the same facial expressions as Monty. He stood there quietly for a second, rubbing his chin before shaking his head slowly.

"No," William said with a smile. "You're a piece of trash and Tristan must be slumming these days to let a stray like you hang about."

"Excuse me?" I asked. "What did you say?"

"Are you deaf as well as dumb?" William replied. "*You* are not his family. I am."

I nearly pulled Grim Whisper and shot him, but LD grabbed my wrist and shook his head. "You can't do that here."

"They're only persuaders. It won't hurt much. I'm only going to shoot him a few times."

"Won't work," LD said, letting go of my arm. "Look around. He's right. We can't blast him."

I narrowed my eyes and saw the multitude of runes inscribed into every surface of the hall. The ones I could make out looked dangerous. Active deterrents against violence with severe consequences. I wasn't in the mood to test my immortality so I slid my hand off Grim Whisper.

"Please, do try," William said. "It won't hurt much."

"Why are you here?" LD asked. "We had you ghosted in China—last I checked."

"I'm a little harder to kill than that," William answered. "But that was a good try."

"Next time I won't miss."

"It's quaint that you think there will be a next time."

"He was here for the Heart," I said, and William narrowed his eyes at me. "Looks like he failed."

"What are you? I mean besides a nuisance?"

"Insightful," I answered. "Am I wrong? You don't look like the monk type. Your attitude demonstrates you're about as enlightened as a broken bulb. That leaves being here for something of value. A mage of your caliber would want the most important and powerful thing here—the White Heart."

"You're not as thick as you seem." He glanced down at Peaches, who rumbled at him. "Is that your creature? What do you feed it?"

"His name is Peaches and he's on a steady diet of uppity mages who think they're superior to everyone else."

William took a step to the side, putting me between him and Peaches. "Duly noted," he said with another glance at my hellhound. "Keep your *Peaches* away from me."

I smiled. "You tried to steal the Heart and they caught your ass."

LD shook his head and chuckled. "I've heard of stupid plans, but this one...amazing. Did you come up with that one on your own or did you have help?"

"My apprentice was with me."

"With Niall?" LD asked in disbelief "You really tried to lift the Heart from *here,* of all places?"

"It was unguarded and no one here can match my ability. It was only a matter of removing it from the time-loop."

"*Only*? From an active time-loop?" LD asked. "Are you insane? You can't possibly be *that* arrogant."

"What happened?" I asked. "I thought no one could match your ability? How did they catch you?"

"My apprentice betrayed me," William answered. "At a crucial moment, he unleashed the wrong rune, debilitating my abilities and alerting the Abbot."

"And left you here," I added. "Why not just create a portal and escape?"

LD shook his head. "He's tethered to Shamballa and the Heart," LD said. "You can't leave...ever."

"What are you talking about?" I asked. "How can he be tethered to the Heart?"

"I'm the Heart's guardian, until I die. The spell Niall unleashed was designed to kill me. I tapped into the power of the Heart to keep myself alive."

"You merged your energy signature," LD said. "It saved your life, but joined you to the Heart."

William nodded. "Permanently."

That explained his diffuse energy signature. He really was all over the place. The White Heart formed part of Shamballa.

"How are we going to borrow the Heart now?"

"You can't *borrow* the Heart," William replied, waving an arm around. "Does this look like a library to you? The Heart is part of the fabric of this place. That's why it's here."

"What's stopping him from taking the Heart and leaving?" I asked, looking at LD. "He can just open a portal and step out."

"He's powerful." LD glanced at William. "He's not 'take the Heart away from Shamballa' powerful."

"So he can check out anytime he wants, but he can never leave?"

"Something like that," LD said with a smile. "He can't even get back to the place he was before."

"Thank you for stating the obvious," William shot back. "In any case, there's only one way the Heart leaves the time-loop and Shamballa."

"How?" I said, dreading the answer I knew was coming.

"I have to come with you."

EIGHTEEN

"HELL NO." I looked at LD. "No way. I don't trust him, I don't like him, and I don't trust him."

"You said that already," LD said.

"That's how much I don't trust him."

"We need to speak to the Abbot," LD answered after a moment. "Maybe there's another way."

"There isn't," William said, waving us to the exit. "But feel free to consult."

A monk approached us from the entrance to the meditation hall. He bowed after giving William a sad look. We returned the bow and the monk spoke.

"Khen Rinpoche will see you now," the monk said. "Please, follow me."

"I'd really just like to punch him in the face," I said as we walked away from a smug-looking William. "He's like the worst version of Monty."

"He's also a few shifts away from being an Archmage," LD said. "Keep that in mind when you unleash your haymaker."

As the monk led us out of the meditation hall, we

crossed several small stone bridges nestled among lush green fields. We followed a path until we arrived at a large lake. Zhuchi stood next to the lake, looking off into the distance. The monk bowed and left us.

"I see you've met the one who needs your help," Zhuchi said. "He carries a deep anger inside"—he glanced at LD—"just like you."

"I'd rather not help him," I said. "He seems like an assh" —I remembered who was I speaking to and course corrected—"a total jerk who will betray us the first chance he gets."

"It's possible," Zhuchi said with a small smile as he gazed into the lake. "It's also possible helping him will help you deal with the difficult choices ahead."

More Yat-ese. At least he didn't carry a staff.

"What choices?" I asked. "Would it be possible to just get a straight answer for once?"

"Every answer you have been given has been at the level of your comprehension," Zhuchi replied, turning to us. "You must deal with your bonds, and you"—he pointed to LD—"must deal with your anger."

"I'm not angry," LD said, quietly looking down at the surface of the lake. "My fury fuels me for what I know must be done."

"What must be done?" I asked. "I didn't get the memo. Why is fury involved in this potentially fatal-sounding plan?"

"You must join the Hearts," Zhuchi said. "This much I have seen."

"I thought we didn't want to join the Hearts?" I looked at LD. "Why are we joining the Hearts?"

"If they're joined, William will be untethered and in

possession of the Gray Heart," LD answered. "We can't trust him. He's the reason Niall is on a rampage."

"And yet," Zhuchi said, turning back to the lake, "you cannot do this without him. You are welcome to leave him and the Heart here and return to your plane."

"No," I said quietly. "We need the Heart to get Monty away from Gabrielle."

"If you give her William, she'll have him *and* the White Heart," LD said. "Tristan may have an opinion about that."

"Then you must choose the greater good over the lesser evil," Zhuchi answered. "Which course of action serves the greatest good?"

"A hint would be good right about now," I said. "Something clear to point us in the right direction?"

"Of course," Zhuchi said with a nod. "Follow the strands of family and friendship. Where they intersect, you will find your answer."

"That wasn't exactly clear. I was thinking more along the lines of 'If you do X, then Y will happen' type of response."

"That's because you are not paying attention," Zhuchi replied. "You have one hour before you must leave, with or without the Heart and its guardian."

"If we remove the Heart, won't it affect this place?" I asked, looking around. "Will it cause damage to Shamballa?"

"In order for it to cause damage, Shamballa would have to be real," Zhuchi answered and started walking away. "And we all know Shamballa is an illusion. I await your choice."

I watched him leave the lake in silence. "I'm pretty

sure Master Yat is one of his students."

"We have to take William," LD said. "If we don't, Gabrielle will kill Tristan."

"If we give him to Psycho Zombie Queen, she'll kill him and give the White Heart to Niall."

"I thought that was the plan?" LD asked. "We give her the White Heart, he comes for the Black Heart, and we stop them."

"That was before the White Heart package came with a tethered mage, who happens to be Monty's brother," I said. "More importantly I'm a little fuzzy on the 'we stop them' part seeing as how the balance of power will be tipped in their favor."

LD nodded and looked off into the distance. "I know."

"I know? What do you mean I know? You're supposed to say 'Don't worry, we got this' or something like 'I'll call in the Ten and we'll wipe them out.' Not 'I know'."

"Don't worry, we got this," LD said with a smile. "Who needs the Ten? We have you, your indestructible hellhound, a misfiring Tristan, and two out the Ten."

"You're going to have to excuse my lack of enthusiasm."

"I'm sure Tristan would like to see his brother again," LD said, clapping me on the shoulder. "Even if it's only to hand over a weapon of destruction to a psychotic Pavormancer bent on erasing us all."

"Anyone ever tell you that your cheerful side is depressing?"

"All the time," LD replied. "Let's go see the Abbot."

NINETEEN

"IS THIS YOUR choice?" Zhuchi asked. "Are you certain about this path?"

"Yes and no," I said.

LD nodded and bowed. "We are."

Zhuchi nodded. He waved a hand and a white stone appeared in his palm a second later. Streamers of bright white energy shot out from the stone and attached it to the ground. Unlike the Black Heart, the White Heart didn't try to crush my skull with a migraine of death.

William approached us, looking at the stone with a mixture of longing and disgust. He kept his distance from the streamers of white energy pulsing into the ground.

Zhuchi waved his hand again. The streamers jumped from the ground and slammed into William, lifting him off his feet and launching him across the grass. The White Heart was gone, but I noticed a faint white energy around William.

"That couldn't have been done gently?" William asked, getting unsteadily to his feet and dusting himself off. He had changed into a dark suit. If he looked like Monty earlier, now he could pass for his older twin.

"Yes," Zhuchi said with a smile. "It could have, but I wanted to remind you, Guardian, of your responsibility now."

"I can assure you, no reminders are necessary," William replied. "I am cognizant of my role here. I am to be the delivery boy and sacrificial lamb. Correct?"

"You're going to save your brother," I said, my voice cold. "Remember? You're his family."

"I'm his family, but I didn't say I'd give my life for his," William answered, his voice colder than mine. "You seem eager to throw your life away. Pity you aren't the one carrying the White Heart. I'd rather enjoy one less fool in this world."

"There's only one fool here and I'm looking at him," I said, managing not to draw Grim Whisper and perforate him.

"What is his ability?" LD asked, looking at Zhuchi. "William was a powerful mage, but now his energy signature is scattered."

"He is still a powerful mage, but his ability to cast and wield magic has been redirected to his purpose with the Heart," Zhuchi said. "If he manages to become unattached from the Heart, he will regain his former abilities."

I saw William nod slightly at Zhuchi's words and knew that was his plan. He would try to find a way to disconnect from the Heart and get his abilities back. He was a time bomb waiting to go off.

I pulled LD to the side. "I don't like this. You know he's going to be looking for a way to break the tether the whole time."

"Exactly," LD answered. "Which makes him predictable. He's going to try and break the tether and keep the power of the Heart for himself. If you know what your enemy is going to do"—LD glanced over at William—"then you can anticipate and plan for it."

"This can go wrong in so many ways," I said, shaking my head. "Even knowing what he's going to do. There are too many variables."

"The alternative is to send you into the Pit without the Heart and see if you can convince Gabrielle to give you Monty."

"That's not much of an alternative."

"Maybe she'll fall victim to your irresistible charisma and you can get Monty back with your suave and debonair repartee?"

"We'll take William."

LD nodded. "Yeah, thought so."

LD gestured and opened a portal. I could see Peck Slip on the other side.

"Thank you again, Khen Rinpoche," LD said with a bow. I copied him and avoided having my ribs massaged by his fist.

Zhuchi returned the bow. "No thanks are necessary," he said. "I believe I have made your life temporarily more difficult."

I looked over at William, who seemed anxious to get through the portal. "I'm going to agree," I said with a nod. "Life has definitely gotten more difficult."

Zhuchi smiled and returned the nod. "For you, Deathless, life is about to get incredibly interesting."

"Right, because my life is so boring," I said, shaking

my head. "I could deal with a few weeks of boring."

Zhuchi gave a short laugh and shook his head. "I'm afraid that, for you, life will never be boring again. Please find a way to come visit again."

A standing invitation to Shamballa by the head Abbot himself? This must be what happens when you leave buildings intact. I made a mental note to share how no temples were harmed or destroyed during my visit.

"Time to go," LD said.

We stepped through the portal and Shamballa disappeared behind us. When I could see clearly again, we were standing in the middle of Peck Slip.

I saw TK standing behind the Dark Goat and gesturing. It looked like she was yelling something, but I couldn't make out the words. She unleashed a large green orb in our direction and pointed behind us. LD shoved me to one side as he cast a lattice around us. I rolled to the ground and drew Grim Whisper. Next to me, Peaches rumbled and entered 'shred and maim' mode.

The next second, a blast of black energy slammed into the lattice, melting it. It was the same kind of energy that destroyed the lobby of Haven. The green orb that TK created deflected the black energy away from us.

"I didn't realize you had become so popular, LD," William said. "It seems like someone would prefer you dead."

"Simon, that's one of Gabrielle's undead mages," LD said, ignoring William. "I'd rather not deal with a zombie mage right now. Do you think you could open your car?"

I looked down the street and saw the revenant. Its hands were covered with black energy and it walked slowly in our direction. This time it was a woman, or what I thought was a woman. It was hard to tell since parts of her were missing.

She had the same grayish complexion, with purple splotches all over what was left of her skin. She shuffled slowly in our direction and I was grateful she was still far away and upwind of us.

"How is Gabrielle managing to control them if she's in Sheol?"

"She's gotten stronger," William said, almost admiringly. "These undead are tracking one of you."

We headed across the street to the Dark Goat. I glanced down one of the side streets and saw a portal open and another one of the undead mages appear. I ran to the driver's side and grabbed the door handle. The entire car flared bright orange for several seconds. I saw runes race along its surface and slowly fade away.

"Tracking us?" I asked. "Those things are undead. How are they tracking anything?"

"Those aren't normal revenants," William said. "She must be using a blood rune."

Peaches jumped into the back and did a semi-sprawl. TK slid in next to him. LD jumped into the passenger side and William stood outside, looking at the Dark Goat, refusing to budge.

"Are you daft? Have you seen the runes on this vehicle?"

"If I remember correctly," I said, "Gabrielle isn't exactly one of your fans. Feel free to stay out here and chat with her undead-mage death squad."

I glanced down another side street and saw another portal open, the third undead mage stepping through. Someone wasn't taking any chances. My real concern was how they'd found us. The third mage was an older man—well, at least looked like an older man. It was hard to tell with the decaying skin and discolorations.

William tugged on one of his sleeves, reminding me of Monty. He walked to the center of Peck Slip.

"What the hell does he think he's doing?" I asked. "Does he think he can deal with three of those things?"

LD shook his head. "Some lessons need to be learned the hard way," he said and looked behind him at TK. "You want this one or should I do the honors?"

TK scratched Peaches behind the ears and waved LD's words away. "The Montagues have always been snobs. Especially in the magic community. I only like Dex, because he never let his ego overshadow his ability."

"Sounds like a no," LD said, getting out of the Goat. "Is that a hard no? Or are you willing to assist?"

"I'm going to surmise that William is here because he has some connection to the White Heart," TK said with a fearsome smile. "Unless you feel this situation is beyond you, dear. My no is adamantine."

"Just asking, darling." LD raised a hand in surrender. "Magical dead zone, three undead mages…figured you'd want to flex some of those casting muscles of yours."

"That's so considerate of you," TK said. "But I'll wait here with Peaches."

She gestured and materialized a sausage, which my

ever-hungry hellhound proceeded to devour.

"Simon, start your beast and let's go make sure William the Arrogant doesn't get blasted to little bits by these mages."

I placed my hand on the dashboard. The engine roared and settled into a purr, vibrating in my gut. I closed my eyes and let in the sensation and sound for a few seconds. The appreciation for automotive artistry was something I always had time for.

LD started gesturing as we closed the distance to William.

"Three undead mages should pose little threat to a mage of my ability," William said. "I will not need your assistance."

"Oh, we're not here to assist," LD said. "More to observe how a mage of your caliber handles this insignificant threat."

"Does he know we're in a magical dead zone?" I asked LD as William took a defensive position. "Will he be able to cast?"

"A mage of his level is always aware of his surroundings," LD replied. "I'm sure he'll find a way around the lack of magic."

"This would only be a dead zone for a lesser mage," William said. "I barely noticed the null effects of this area. I hardly think it will impact my ability to cast."

I raised an eyebrow and shook my head. I took a deep breath and let my senses expand. William's energy signature was strong, but scattered. I wondered what the lack of focus meant when it came to the actual casting.

LD glanced at me and then looked down at my mala

bracelet. I understood the unspoken message. I made sure my shield was ready.

"Are you sure you're going to be able to handle all three?" I asked. "You may be a little out of practice."

"Out of practice?" William scoffed. "I'm two shifts away from being an Archmage. I'm a Montague. I can't expect you to understand since whatever magic you possess is negligible."

I saw TK step outside of the Dark Goat. She narrowed her eyes at William and then caught LD's attention, giving him a short shake of her head. They had been together so long that they had developed an unspoken language.

LD took a step closer to me, and we both moved back a few feet from William. "Pay attention, Simon. You're going to see a Montague in action."

"You realize I get to see Monty in action all the time, right?"

"Yes, but this is different."

"Wouldn't it be better if we just jumped in the Goat and left the zombie mages behind?"

"Are you always this much of a coward?" William gestured and white trails of energy followed his movements. "Montagues don't run. We make our enemies run."

"Arrogant and stupid," I said under my breath. "Is he trying to get himself killed?"

"It's better if we stop them here," LD said. "We don't want to run into them on the Hell Gate. I think once we make it across, we'll have our hands full."

"Adding undead mages would be a bit much, true."

"Be ready to move," LD said. "I have a feeling the

White Heart is going to make things difficult."

TWENTY

THE UNDEAD FEMALE mage in the center formed a large orb of black energy and released it into the air above her. The other two mages had shambled close to her and did the same, joining their orbs to hers.

The two mages on the side were casting black runes into the air while the center female mage maintained the integrity of the new orb. I had a flashback of the orb that destroyed our first Goat.

"LD, I don't think we want to be in direct line of that thing," I said, making sure I had access to my mala bead. "If Gabrielle is somehow controlling these things, mages or zombies or whatever they are, does it make sense that the magic that they're using is necromancy?"

LD nodded. "That orb is looking pretty nasty," he said as he pulled me away from William and closer to the Goat. "Are you sure you have this under control, William?"

The sun was setting. In an hour or so, we weren't going to be able to see anything. The magical dead zone had made it nearly impossible to run any power to this block. Apparently, magical dead zones didn't work well with electricity.

"Feel free to run to the vehicle," William replied. "I'll make short work of these creatures."

He finished gesturing and formed an orb of white energy. With a word under his breath, he unleashed it at the black orb. The white orb raced forward and smashed into the orb over the undead mage's head. The shockwave washed over us, nearly knocking us down.

For a few brief seconds, Peck Slip was illuminated by the explosion of a mini sun, temporarily blinding me and making it impossible to track the undead mages.

William turned back and looked at us smugly, putting his hands on his hips. "*That*, is how you deal with lesser creatures," he said with a sneer. "Poor wretches never stood a chance."

Once my vision returned to normal, I looked up the street. Before I saw it, I could sense the dark energy rushing at us. I pressed the center bead on my mala bracelet. My shield materialized, but I knew it wasn't going to be enough.

"That's a lot of angry nastiness headed this way, LD," I said. "I'd rather not try and deflect it with my shield."

William looked at me as confusion flitted across his face.

"What are you talking about?" William turned and saw the impending orb of destruction headed our way. To his credit, he reacted well. He formed several orbs of white flame in his hand and unleashed them. They bounced off the black orb and smashed into the surrounding buildings, ripping chunks of brick and stone with every impact.

"You may want to head to the car right about now," I said as I drew Grim Whisper and switched the magazine to entropy rounds. "Those *lesser creatures* are headed this way and I don't think your orbs of wonder and light are going to do anything to them."

William stood there, looking down at his hands for a few seconds. "I know I used the right spell," he muttered to himself. "It was the spell of dissolution. That should've finished them."

"Now!" yelled LD. "William, get to the car, now."

William shook himself out of his reverie and ran for the Goat.

"Are you going to be able to stop that thing?" I asked as the black orb descended on us. "The last time I saw something like this, a magistrate melted the Goat. I'm not crazy about being slagged into a puddle today."

"Headshots," LD said, creating a lattice of gray energy. "Don't waste time shooting them in the body."

"Got it." I took aim and fired at the female mage, placing an entropy round in the center of her forehead. She flew back several feet before bursting into a mound of dust. The other two mages formed several smaller black orbs and sent them our way. "We have incoming."

"Kind of busy at the moment," LD said. I could hear the strain in his voice as a lattice he created caught the black orb. "Nice of you to come see how we're doing, darling."

"Excuse me?" I said. "I know we're friendly, but we're not *that* friendly."

"Wasn't talking to you," LD answered with a grunt. "Do you think you could do something about the orbs headed our way?"

"I don't think entropy rounds are going to do much to those orbs," I said, still confused. "You want me to shoot them?"

"Of course, dear," TK said, appearing behind me, nearly startling me into a heart attack. She gave me a short nod when I noticed her.

"How did you—? Weren't you just in the Dark Goat?"

TK nodded and gave me a smile I could only describe as sinchievous. I was beginning to realize that most of the qualities she exhibited were just this side of sinister.

I was grateful that she hadn't completely stepped over to the dark side. I'd hate to face an evil TK. I remembered the Reckoning and made a mental note not to face TK, period.

"It was either come out here or stay in the car with *him*," she said. "He kept muttering something about using the correct spell, but the Heart obstructed his power."

TK had managed to exit the Goat and walk up behind us without my sensing her. I thought she was dangerous before, but her stealth mode meant that she could mask herself into virtual invisibility. I glanced at her and realized she had all the skills of a master assassin.

Even scarier, LD had sensed her when I couldn't. These two were in a league beyond what I could comprehend.

"Hun?" LD asked and gestured with his head. "Think you could clear a path for Simon?"

TK nodded and swept an arm horizontally in front

of her body. The incoming orbs imploded several feet away from us.

"Path cleared," she said. "Would you like some more help?"

"Thanks, no," I said, marveling at the effortlessness of her gesture. "I can take it from here."

I ran forward with Grim Whisper in my hand. The growl next to me brought a smile to my face as I saw my black hole of a hellhound blink in and keep pace next to me.

<Can I bite them?>

<I don't think they'll taste good.>

<After your magic meat, how bad could they be?>

<They're undead so they're rotting and probably filled with nasty infections. Don't bite them.>

<Was your meat undead-meat? Is that why it was bad?>

<My meat was excellent you just have no taste. You can hit them, but don't bite them.>

<Your meat broke my taste, too. Is that why I have no taste?>

Peaches blinked out and landed on one of the undead mages with enough force to shatter the cobblestones in the street. The mage never stood a chance and burst into dust a second later. I fired Grim Whisper and put down the other mage, who reverted to dust before Peaches could barrel into him.

I turned to let TK and LD know the mages were dispatched and re-dead. LD had trapped the large black orb in the lattice. I could see he was struggling with keeping it in place. With a nod, he motioned to TK, who gestured, blasting a shaft of green energy through the orb, dispersing it into a thin black cloud that disappeared.

"That is how that's done," I said, heading down the street when a wave of energy slammed into me, doubling me over with a gasp. I placed a hand on the cobblestone street to steady myself and noticed the frost forming around my fingers.

"Simon, run!" LD yelled as he ran toward me. TK traced runes in the air, forming a green lattice over the Dark Goat, and trapping William inside.

The roar of crashing waves filled my ears as the cold grip of fear froze me in place. I could see LD yelling something else at me, but the explosion of sound drowned out his voice. My vision started tunneling in and I saw LD recede into the distance. Peck Slip had suddenly become several miles long.

"What the hell?" I muttered, looking at Peaches, who was facing behind me in 'pounce and trounce' mode. "Run, boy. Get to the car."

I started turning in the direction of the energy, when another wave embraced me. This one was different. I sensed it approach tentatively, closing the distance slowly and wrapping itself around me like a body scarf.

My hand started shaking so violently I barely managed to holster Grim Whisper. All around us, dozens of dark portals appeared.

<Bad things are coming. They smell like home.>

<At least you didn't say you see dead people. I can't move, boy.>

My breath formed a small cloud in front of my face as I gasped again. The sensation of extreme cold squeezed my chest, constricting my breathing. I tried to stand, but my legs had gone on strike and refused to budge.

I struggled to look up and saw LD in the distance, still running toward me. I tried moving, but my body refused to respond. Every cell in my brain was screaming "run," but all my muscles were curled up in the fetal position, gibbering in fear.

<Get...away...boy. This...is...bad.>

Peaches stepped close to me and whined. He nudged me with his head and I knew he was being gentle because I wasn't launched across the street.

<I smell a bad man coming. You have to run.>

<I can't. My body won't move. I'm...I'm too scared.>

<I will help you.>

A searing pain shot up my arm as my hellhound clamped down on my hand. The immediate pain removed the paralyzing fog of fear. I staggered to my feet and stumbled down the street, toward the Dark Goat.

<You had to bite me? Why didn't you use your healing saliva?>

<Are you hurt?>

<You mean besides the wounds you just inflicted in my hand?>

<I was being gentle. You still have your fingers.>

My body flushed with heat as the wounds sealed and repaired themselves. I drew Grim Whisper and turned to the source of terror behind me.

A tall thin man dressed in a long coat walked down the street. His blue-black hair, cut short, contrasted against his pale glowing skin in the dying light of the day. He looked at me with a thin smile across his lips. Around him, dark shadow-like figures emerged from the portals.

"Those don't look friendly," I muttered, stepping back. "I think I prefer the undead mages to this."

"You managed to break my fearcasting?" the man said, narrowing his eyes at me. "How did you do this?"

I wasn't going to tell him it took hand mangling by my hellhound to break out of his spell. Trade secrets and all.

"I'm stronger than I look," I said, shaking out my freshly injured hand. "Probably can kick your ass if I tried."

He smiled, fixed me with his gaze, and took a deep breath. "Lies. I can smell your fear from here," he said, licking his lips, officially creeping me out. "It smells delicious."

"First, gross," I said as he approached. "Second, I'm just going to go on the record and say that Pavormancy sucks. I'm guessing you must be Niall?"

"Indeed," he answered. "Where is my old teacher? Where is William? I sense his energy signature close and I have so much pain to share before I destroy him."

"Tall, cranky mage with a raging superiority complex?"

Niall nodded. "Give him to me. He has what I require."

"Never heard of him," I said, shaking my head slowly. "What you require is therapy. You should really go back home."

"Home?" Niall snapped. Judging from the extra dose of crazy I saw in his eyes, mentioning home was a bad idea. "I can never go home. His betrayal cost me everything."

"His betrayal?" I asked, trying to buy time to shake off the effects of being scared shitless. "He betrayed you?"

Someone was playing loose and fast with the truth. I had a feeling it wasn't the Angry Goth Pavormancer who was twisting his words. For a split second, I was tempted to give him William. If I did, Gabrielle would leave Monty in Sheol. That wasn't going to happen while I was still breathing.

"I will not explain myself to you. Give him to me or die."

"You're going to find that last part a little difficult."

"You dare mock me? Do you know who I am?"

"The question is: do I care? The answer? Not really."

Peaches growled and bared his teeth.

<No, boy. We need to get to the car and get away from him.>

"William isn't here and whatever it is you *need*, isn't here either." I tried sounding convincing. If he was a virtual fear detector, there was a good chance he would see right through me. "Maybe he's stuck in some far off land where—"

"You are a terrible liar," he said, holding up a hand and sniffing the air. "The stink of fear betrays you. I sense his energy signature. More importantly…I smell his fear."

"No, sorry, what you're smelling is the residue of the healthy sausage I made for my hellhound," I said, patting down my jacket. "The smell refuses to leave."

Niall stood still and looked around. His gaze settled on the Dark Goat and he pointed. "There," he said quietly. "He's there."

I raised Grim Whisper and aimed. "Cecil is real

touchy about who destroys the Dark Goat," I said. "Why don't you turn around and go back to whatever dark dimension you crawled out of?"

Niall unleashed another wave of frigid cold. Its suddenness made me shudder. I fired Grim Whisper, emptying the magazine. Nothing happened. Except now I faced an upset Pavormancer.

"Shit, plan B."

<*What's plan B? Bite starts with B. Is this the plan where I bite him?*>

<*Plan B is where we run to the Dark Goat and get away from this freak.*>

Niall cocked his head to one side, glaring at me. "You should be on the ground removing your entrails with your bare hands." He narrowed his eyes and formed an orb of black energy. "Who are you?"

"No one of consequence," I said, stepping back down Peck Slip and closer to the Dark Goat. My body had regained its mobility, but I felt the undercurrent of fear ratcheting up in my stomach. The orb in his hand looked angry and dangerous. Arcs of violet light raced around the orb as it floated in his hand.

"Humor me," he said with a nod. "I'd like to know how you managed to break my casting before I kill you."

"Get used to disappointment," I said and dashed for the Dark Goat. Peaches blinked out and reappeared in the back seat. LD and TK unleashed orbs of their own and launched them at Niall.

"Kill them."

Those were the last words I heard before the orbs collided with Niall and set off another explosion of light.

TWENTY-ONE

I JUMPED INTO the Dark Goat and pulled the door closed. The shadow figures raced at us and slammed the side of the car, rocking the vehicle. I left them behind as I stepped on the gas and sped off. In the rear-view mirror, I saw another black orb leave the unscathed Niall's hands.

"Those orbs didn't even scratch him," I said. "I think he's sending us a going away present."

"I think," TK said, calmly, "we will get to experience firsthand how effective Cecil is with his runes."

The orb Niall released raced along the ground, disintegrating cobblestones as it closed on us.

"Shit, it's another Goat Melter," I said. "Can any of you stop that thing?"

"Goat Melter?" William asked, looking around. "There are no animals in here except for this large creature you call a dog"—he slid away from Peaches —"if he even qualifies as part of the species."

"His name is Peaches and he's a hellhound," I said, my voice hard. "My hellhound. If you keep irritating me I'll let him bite you."

<*He probably tastes bad. No, thank you.*>

<*You're right. I wouldn't torture you like that.*>

<*Thank you. When you get a chance, can you have the scary lady make me some meat?*>

<*I'm a little busy right now, how about later?*>

<*How much later? I'm getting hungry.*>

<*I'm trying to avoid getting melted by that ball of energy behind us. Can you stop it?*>

<*You do know I'm not a mage? Maybe I can bite it?*>

<*Right, so let me focus on keeping us in one piece. If we get away from this thing, we can focus on meat.*>

<*That's the problem, you focus on other things besides meat. Meat is life.*>

LD had turned to look at the incoming orb. "Simon, you need to go faster. Like *much* faster."

I jumped on to the FDR and glanced in the rear-view mirror again. The orb was much closer now.

"Can't you cast an anti-disintegration spell or something that will keep that thing from melting the Goat?"

"Not from in here," LD answered, opening a window. "The surface runes used by Cecil prevent any casting. Hun?"

TK traced some runes in the air. They fizzled out in less than three seconds. "Too much runic interference."

"If you were a higher class of mage—" William started and went silent when he looked at TK.

"You do not want to finish that sentence." LD looked at William and shook his head.

"There's too much runic interference," TK restated, looking at William. "Please feel free to use your greatly diminished powers to stop a necromantic orb sent to melt this vehicle."

"Well, when you put it that way, I'm sure—"

"I'm going to try something from out here." LD gestured and launched a series of gray runes at the orb. It seemed to slow down and then pick up speed again.

"That kind of worked," I said. "It looked like it was attached to a rubber band. It slowed down and then snapped back after us."

"It's probably tethered to William somehow," LD said. "If it's not tethered, it's tracking his energy signature. Darling, can we cast a mimic?"

TK nodded and grabbed a handful of William's hair. "This is going to hurt you more than it's going to hurt me," she said and yanked, pulling a tuft of hair out of his head.

"Bloody hell!" William yelled, rubbing his head. He calmed down immediately when Peaches rumbled, looking at him. "Are you insane, woman?"

"Yes." TK gestured with one hand and let William's hair fall into the runes she was tracing. They disintegrated and turned the runes a bright red. She pushed her hand forward and passed the runes to LD, who cast a gray orb around it.

With the red runes encased in the orb, LD stuck half his body out of the window and cast the orb over the side of the FDR into the East River. The black orb changed direction and followed the gray orb into the water. A few seconds later a muffled explosion shot a massive column of water into the sky.

"Tethered," LD said, looking over the side of the FDR. "If his shadowform has your energy signature, you are FUBAR."

TK nodded. "William, is it possible Niall acquired your energy signature?" she asked. "Your blood, perhaps?"

William gave a quick glance out of the rear window. The column of water was still rising into the air.

"A distinct possibility," he said with a nod. "We're fortunate we aren't facing his true form."

"True form?" I asked, speeding up the highway. "What do you mean 'true form'?"

William sighed. "Niall is a Pavormancer. A gifted one at that. When his ability was discovered, I convinced the Golden Circle to choose preservation over erasure, due to its rarity."

"That didn't work out so well," I said, swerving around cars. "I get that mages enjoy living dangerously, but no one thought this was a bad idea?"

"Tristan dissented. Along with a small group of mages. The Elders ignored them and listened to me."

"Let me guess, those that dissented have all been retired?"

"Permanently. Pavormancers can project shadowforms of themselves," William said. "What we faced earlier was his shadowform. Had we been facing the real Niall, we wouldn't be here to have this discussion."

"Monty said you went dark and took several mages with you. Niall was one of them."

"Over time Niall changed. His darker nature emerged and he started using his ability to kill."

"Wonder where that influence came from?"

"I may have gone dark," William shot back, "but I'm

not evil."

"Said every evil mage, ever."

"Believe what you will," William said, waving my words away. "I tried to stop him."

"Stop him? Stop him from what?"

"Niall started seeking the forbidden texts. He became desperate for power."

"This just gets better by the second." I glanced at William in the rear-view mirror. "Why didn't you kill him?"

"*Kill* him? A Pavormancer?" William replied, upset. "A discipline we hadn't seen in centuries and those myopic Elders wanted to erase it. We could have studied it, learned from it."

"Some disciplines are best left unstudied."

"My uncle felt the same way and summoned these two"—he motioned to TK and LD with a hand —"along with their band of misfits. They interfered and stopped us. I thought Niall dead after that."

"I thought we ghosted them in China," LD said, looking at William. "Should've checked for bodies. Damn Gabrielle."

I glanced over at LD. "She faked their deaths?"

LD nodded. "The situation in Asia was fluid and lethal at the time," he said. "She's a necromancer and masked their signatures to make it appear that they had died. I won't make the same mistake twice."

"What were you doing in China?"

"Tibet, actually," William answered. "Before the Ten stopped him in Asia, Niall had discovered the location of five of the lost runes."

"Only two have ever been found," LD said. "We've

all looked. The other three are truly lost."

"Lost runes?" I asked. "That's what Yat was looking for."

"Earth, Air, Water, Fire, and Void," William said. "Each one corresponds to a discipline...and each one was given solid form."

"The Black Heart is Void?" I asked, shaking my head. "How do mages create these items of immense power and then *lose* them? That makes the White Heart...?"

"...Fire," William answered. "Affecting every spell with a flame component."

"I thought these were temporal runes affecting time?"

"They are, but specifically Void deals with time and space," William answered. "Any of the five can be joined to the Void rune."

Then it dawned on me. "Can they all be joined together? All five?"

William stared at me for a few seconds. "That is quite an intuitive question. Niall asked me the same thing before he embarked on his cause."

"He mentioned *you* betrayed him. Care to clarify why he would say that?"

"I may have obfuscated the details slightly about the events in Shamballa," William said quietly. "He was about to abscond with the White Heart and destroy Shamballa in the process."

"You stopped him?"

"No, I've merely delayed him." William looked out of the window. "You intend to give him the White Heart, in exchange for Tristan. Correct?"

"Correct," I said, my voice as soft as granite. "I'm

not leaving Monty to the Zombie Queen, and honestly, you caused most of this shitstorm. Make your bed, lie in it."

"Your eloquence is astounding," William muttered. "No wonder my brother enjoys your company so."

"The White Heart isn't the lynchpin, it's the Black Heart," I said as other thoughts fell into place. "What happens if all the runes are joined?"

"No one alive is powerful enough to join them all," LD said. "Even if they could find them."

"That's the source, isn't it?" I asked. "All five make the source of magic."

William shook his head slowly. "Close, but there is an important distinction," William answered. "The five runes aren't the source of magic. Joining all five *create* the source of magic."

"I don't understand."

"I doubt you could," William answered. "You're not a mage, offense intended."

"Just when I thought you were somewhat civilized, you revert to being an ass," I said and saw the sign informing us that the Randalls Island exit was a mile away. "Make it easy to understand for us simpleminded folk."

"The five lost runes convert the caster *into* a source of magic," LD said. "Basically, whoever can find all five runes, join them, and then trigger the energy contained inside each one without blowing themselves apart, becomes a god."

"This is what Niall wants?" I asked. "You were helping him achieve this?"

"No." William stared at me through the mirror. "I

wasn't helping *him.*"

"Fuck me," I whispered under my breath as I made the connection. "You weren't helping him. He was helping *you.*"

"Your powers of deductive reasoning are exceptional for someone of such low intelligence," William said with a smile. "I look forward to our next meeting. Please give my regards to what's left of Tristan."

"Stop him!" I yelled.

William shoved Peaches into TK, kicked open the door next to him before any of us could react, and leaped out of the Dark Goat into the East River.

TWENTY-TWO

I SCREECHED TO a stop on the FDR, nearly causing several collisions. I jumped out of the Dark Goat and looked around, but William was gone.

"Where did he go?" I asked, looking around and expecting to see a bloody smear on the lower roadway where he should have landed. "How did he——?"

"Once he was out of the vehicle, the inhibiting runes no longer stopped his casting." TK looked over the edge and narrowed her eyes. "He's gone. I don't sense his signature in the area."

"I should've let Peaches bite him, maybe remove a leg or two," I said, feeling the anger rise in my chest. "How did I miss it?"

"Why would you torture your hellhound that way?" she said as we got back inside the Dark Goat. "That would be worse than that meat you created for him."

"It was a setup," I said, banging both hands on the wheel. "He played us like amateurs."

"It doesn't make sense," LD said. "The Abbot at Shamballa wouldn't help him do this."

"Is the Abbot human?" I asked. "Seriously."

"Of course, he's human," LD replied. "What kind of question is—?"

"Then he's corruptible. William got to him somehow."

"The Abbot of Shamballa?" LD asked, shaking his head. "Are you crazy?"

"I suggest we get moving before we attract more attention," TK said, looking at the crowd of cars forming behind us. The horns of the angry drivers formed a chorus of irritation. I started the Dark Goat and pulled away.

"You said no one alive could join all the runes," I said as the wheels in my head kept turning. "Right? It would blast whoever tried to little bits."

"It's too much power," LD answered. "You felt the Black Heart, imagine that magnified exponentially, each stone being a factor of ten."

"I remember it wanted to crush my brain. With extreme pain."

LD nodded. "By the time the final stone was in place and the last rune cast, your brain would be a puddle."

"What if the person joining them isn't alive?" I asked slowly as the pieces fell into place. "What if the person who joins the rune is dead? William has a necromancer."

"Stop the car," TK said with urgency. "Stop the car —now."

"Hun, what's going on?" LD asked, concerned. "His driving isn't that bad."

"He's right." TK jumped out of the Dark Goat, gestured, and formed a portal. "The White Heart will lead William to Fordey. I need to move the Black Heart, now."

"I'm going with you," LD said and began gesturing. "It's too dangerous for you to do this alone. For all we know, William is at full power or worse, enhanced with the White Heart."

TK rested a hand gently on LD's arm and stopped him. "You have to go with Simon. Tristan needs help."

"Let him take the hellhound express," LD replied quickly. "No offense, hombre but, in terms of priority, this lady is my breath."

"None taken," I said, raising my hand surrender. "I'm sure Peaches and I can find a way."

"No," TK said, shutting down further argument. "Get them into the Pit, then come and help me."

"Hun," LD said, shaking his head. "I don't like this at all."

"I know." TK pressed a hand against LD's cheek. "I'll try to leave the Danger Room intact. Hurry up and follow me."

TK stepped through the portal and disappeared. LD set his jaw, giving all the cars whose drivers started honking again the one-finger salute, and jumped into the Dark Goat. I pulled away before the police showed up.

TWENTY-THREE

"WHAT KIND OF defenses are we looking at?" I asked, looking across the Hell Gate Bridge. "Are they going to try and explode us on approach?"

The Hell Gate Bridge was a railroad bridge used to transport goods into the city. When not used for prison transport to Sheol, it doubled as a materials transport to different parts of the city. Most of the time it remained closed.

The railways had been removed decades earlier and replaced with roads to allow for vehicular crossing. That was all the information I could gather on the Hell Gate Bridge without digging deeper and attracting the wrong kind of attention.

The drive to the bridge approach had been a quiet one as LD kept mostly silent. That nimbus of fury he kept in check was barely contained as he undid his seatbelt. The runes in the Dark Goat pulsed with energy as we stepped out and looked across the span.

Peaches nudged me and nearly sent me over the edge of the bridge.

<You need to nudge softer, or maybe not nudge at all? I can hear you, you know.>

<Sometimes the nudge is easier. You don't always hear me clearly.>

<What are you talking about? I hear you all the time.>

<You didn't listen when I said don't make the magic meat.>

<Are you going to drop it?>

<I wish I had, before I ate it.>

I shook my head realizing this was a losing battle.

<What do you want?>

<Does the scary angry man need me to lick him? My saliva can calm him down.>

<Oh sure, him you lick, but you bite me.>

<He's angry, not scared. Should I lick him?>

<No, don't lick him. He's worried about TK, the scary lady.>

<Why? She's stronger than he is.>

<She's his mate. He doesn't want her to get hurt.>

<I'm sure he doesn't make undead sausages for her.>

<I need you to focus. We have to cross this bridge and then go into a bad place and get Monty.>

<Will he make me meat after we get him out?>

<You need to focus on the priority here.>

<I am. Meat is always the priority.>

"There aren't going to be any defenses by the time we get to the alignment location," LD said quietly. "I'll remove all the obstacles and get you inside. You get Tristan out of the Pit, dead or alive."

"What do you mean dead or alive?"

"Did I stutter?" LD shot back. "Whatever state he's in, you get him out of the Pit."

"Got it," I said.

A cold knot of fear settled in my stomach. I never thought Monty might not survive in the Pit. It was my idea to go to Shamballa first. If that delay caused Monty's—I didn't want to think about it. I pushed the thoughts out of my head and focused on the bridge.

"Once you're out, head to the back room of the neutral location near your home. Do not go home or anywhere else except that room. Is that clear?"

"Crystal?" I asked, confused. "What about Gabrielle? I'm going to have to face her in there."

LD shook his head. "Gabrielle and her undead are with Niall and William, probably trying to get through Fordey's defenses this very moment."

"What do you mean? This is where she brought Monty."

"She brought him here, but she didn't stay here. We faced undead mages at Peck Slip. There's no way she can summon and control undead mages and be in Sheol simultaneously."

"She was controlling the mages on Peck Slip."

LD nodded. "She can mask her signature to appear dead. She left Tristan here because he was the greatest threat to William."

"And then manipulated us into getting the White Heart," I said. "William was being held in Shamballa. We helped him get out."

"It's beginning to look that way," he said. "I should have roasted their asses in China. I shouldn't have held back."

"She brought Monty here not knowing about his abilities being compromised or the shift he's going through."

LD nodded. "That worked out for them," he said. "If Tristan were at full strength, then I would be at Fordey right now with TK."

"I'm sure TK will be—"

LD shut me up with a look. "Simon, it's all I can manage to keep from blowing this bridge to debris so I can go be with her," he said, his voice slicing through the night. "Park the car off the bridge and follow behind me on the path so you can activate the priming runes. Stay behind me until we cross to the other side."

I moved the Dark Goat to a side street and locked it with the familiar clang of metal and orange flare of runes across its surface. Black energy wafted up for a few seconds, and then it blended into the background, disappearing from sight.

I ran back to where LD stood. The energy came off him in waves and I was thankful he and I weren't enemies. When I'd first met him, I didn't understand what TK saw in him. I understood now and it scared the hell out of me.

LD formed two gray orbs laced with black energy and ran across the bridge. Armed guards rushed out to meet him and he greeted them with orbs and fury. His restraint in not killing them only spoke to his amazing control. None of the guards withstood the devastation of his attacks.

Every time we passed one of the structural pylons on the bridge, a large rune glowed underneath our feet, bathing us in a wash of energy that made my hair stand on end.

We got to the other side and faced a large brick wall. LD narrowed his eyes and felt around the wall for a few seconds. He moved quickly and efficiently.

He gestured again, this time taking a little longer. I recognized some of the runes as the symbols Ronin had showed him.

A large metal double door formed in the brick wall. The entrance was large enough to drive a small van or medium-sized truck through.

"This will take me to Monty?"

"This will take you to the Pit. Tristan should be close."

"Thank you," I said. "I'll meet you at the Rump."

"This is not a tour, Simon. Get in, get Tristan, and get out. Remember, no curse to keep your ass alive in the Pit."

I nodded and pulled on the door. It opened with little resistance. That didn't surprise me considering how difficult it was to even get the door to appear.

I turned to see LD gesture, create a portal, and disappear. I almost felt sorry for whoever dared attack Fordey and TK. They had no idea the level of destruction that was heading fast and furious to Fordey.

TWENTY-FOUR

I STEPPED INSIDE Sheol with Peaches by my side.

The runes on the threshold burst with orange light, casting stark shadows as we crossed into a large open area with only one exit. I looked down a long, empty corridor.

Everything around us was done in various expressions of drab gray concrete. I could smell the faint scent of ammonia in the air. It reminded me of a hospital, if hosptials were made of poured concrete, were depressing, and were supermax magical prisons. I turned around and saw the door we had used to enter had vanished. A large "P1" was stenciled on the wall in its place.

We were on the first level of the Pit.

I narrowed my eyes and examined the room. Every surface contained runes. Some I understood, warnings and inhibitors. Others, I couldn't decipher—probably instant death and maiming the moment you crossed the exit.

I walked to the edge of the doorway in front of me

and peered through without crossing the threshold. There were five stacked levels including the one I stood on. Each level was connected by ramps on either end of the short side of the rectangle.

Around the long arm of the rectangle, I could see five metal doors on either side. Angry red runes covered each one. The Pit only housed fifty cells and Monty was inside one of them.

<This place feels bad.>

<This place is bad. Can you feel Monty?>

Peaches stood still and smelled the air. I let my senses expand and immediately came up against a runic wall of power blocking me. I was surprised by the fact that I could still sense energy signatures. That surprise turned to the sudden realization that my senses didn't extend past the doorway. I tried looking into the center of the levels. Past the lowest level, I only saw darkness. We were in some kind of abyss, which explained why they called this place the Pit.

I picked up motion on the platform one level below us and backed away from the doorway fast, pulling Peaches with me. I knew I had to be scared, because I actually managed to pull him back several feet.

<Stay here. I need to check something.>

I stepped slowly to the doorway and peeked around the edge. After about a minute of looking, I saw them. Large monstrous creatures patrolled each of the levels. They each carried a rune-covered flail with three nasty-looking spiked balls, each at the end of a long chain. The last time I had seen one of these creatures, I was on a doomed date with Katja.

The one on my level was easily eight feet tall and half

as wide. Any larger and he would've had his own zip code. He was shirtless with deep, red pulsing runes covering his torso. I didn't understand how something so large could move so silently.

I was staring at a Troll.

This explained the ramps at the end of each level. Trolls didn't navigate stairs well. They usually just destroyed them on the way down, or up, but it made sense.

If you needed to keep magical prisoners under control, Trolls were the perfect guards. They were resistant to magic even indirectly and had only one weak point; the eyes.

<We have Trolls in there.>

<Trolls smell very bad.>

<Trolls are monsters that are hard to stop. Magic doesn't stop them.>

<That's okay, your magic is not very strong. Maybe you can make them some magic meat and hurt their stomachs?>

I stared at my hellhound and shook my head. This should be easy. All I needed was a soul render—a weapon designed to exploit their weakness, and maybe an army.

The last time I faced a Troll, I had Monty, Chi, and Katja with her dagger. This time it was just me and my hungry hellhound. My Grim Whisper and Ebonsoul would probably give the first troll I encountered a severe case of the giggles, right before he smashed a fist into my head, squashing it.

I was running out of options and time. Peaches padded over and bumped me gently with his head shoving me into the wall.

<I can smell the angry man and monsters.>

<How far away is Monty?>

The odds of Gabrielle placing Monty on the first level of the Pit were slim to none, but I could hope.

<He is down. Under us two times.>

<Under us, two times? How many monsters do you smell?>

<Five monsters.>

Monty was on the third level. Getting there without attracting the attention of the two trolls above and below would require us to be invisible. A hellhound with glowing red eyes was low on the subtlety scale.

<We have to go get Monty, but I'm going to need you to run interference.>

<Interference? Is that like when you destroy a building we are in?>

<I destroy? Last time I checked, I wasn't the nearly indestructible hellhound or super powerful mage.>

<The angry man said you have a reputation. You are dangerous. Are people scared of you?>

<We're going to need your battlemode.>

There was only one problem. The entropy collar acted as a limiter to prevent him from becoming Peaches XL. I still didn't know how to work around it. To access Planet Peaches, his collar and my bracelet needed to be gone.

<Boy, you're going to need to get bigger.>

<Bigger would call the monsters.>

<I know. You're going to call the monsters. I'm going to find Monty. When I do, you come to me.>

<The monsters will come too.>

<You'll have to get there first.>

<How will I get big? The magic band around my neck won't

let me.>

<We're going to need help taking it off.>

Peaches looked around the room and chuffed.

<No one else is here.>

<Move to the corner and give me a moment.>

Peaches stepped over to the corner and sat on his haunches, staring at me.

<If you make your magic meat and give it to them, it will break their stomachs and we can get the angry man.>

<I'm not risking any meat. One gastric meltdown from you was enough. Step back. I'm going to call help...I think.>

I pressed my mark and held my breath. White light shot out from the top of my left hand. Everything around me became slightly out of focus and frozen.

I wasn't sure she would show, especially in a magical null zone like Sheol. A small part of me wished she wouldn't. I was getting used to not having my skull rattled by her delicate facial taps, but I needed her help. It was the only way I could think of getting the collar off.

The heady smell of lotus blossoms filled my lungs as I took a deep breath. The complex scent was laden with citrus and mixed with an enticing hint of cinnamon. This was followed by the sweet smell of wet earth after a hard rain.

A woman appeared a few feet away and stared at me. My heart seized for a split-second as the cloud of violet energy around her dissipated. The power I sensed around her was difficult to comprehend. She cocked her head to one side and looked around.

"Splinter," she said, "have you finally decided to incarcerate yourself for the good of the populace?"

She was dressed in a dark blue robe with a repeated flying crane print. It flowed around her as if caught in a gentle breeze. Her hair was loose and flowed with the same breeze that moved the robe.

Beneath the robe, she wore a loose-fitting white blouse and a black mini-skirt. Blazoned on the side of the robe was a large letter B. Black ankle boots with heels that were weapons in their own right finished the ensemble.

Strapped across her back was a naginata, or glaive. She removed it, swung it around her body in one fluid movement, and stopped the blade less than an inch away from my neck. I kept still. The blade looked sharp enough to cut through reality.

"Why am I here?" she said, holding the blade perfectly still.

"Hello, Karma," I said. I knew how she felt about being summoned.

"Decapitating you would rid me of countless headaches," she said, letting the blade touch my skin lightly. I felt the blood drip down my neck from the wound. "What do you want?"

Her hazel eyes gleamed with power even in this place. I knew better than to gaze into her eyes. She looked female, but Karma was the personification of causality. Staring into her eyes would fry my brain in seconds.

"Monty is in here and I need to get him out."

"What's this?" she said, looking around the space and waving a hand. "Extreme minimalist?"

"I need your help."

She removed the naginata and absorbed it into one hand. With the grace of a dancer, she closed the distance and stood next to me. My breath caught in my lungs and refused to leave my body.

The fear I felt with Niall was a lover's caress compared to this. She placed the back of her hand against one of my cheeks and flicked her wrist, sending me sailing across the floor.

"*That* was for summoning me. I told you I'm not a genie you can summon without consequence."

Spots danced in my vision as I staggered to my feet. If this was what it took to help Monty, so be it. The sheer scope of her power was unimaginable as the floor shifted under my feet.

"I need your help," I said again, trying to maintain my balance. "I wouldn't have done this otherwise."

"No. I can't help you without disrupting causality," she answered, examining her fingernails. "I thought I explained this to you. Helping you only creates other situations I must deal with. I can't alter cause and effect."

She crossed her arms over her chest, daring me to refute her.

"Bullshit," I said, figuring that if I was going to die, it was a good last word. I would've said "rosebud," but that wouldn't have made sense. "You *can* help."

She narrowed her eyes and came close again. "Splinter," she said sweetly, that one word carrying enough menace to freeze my blood, "are you calling me a liar? To my face?"

In for a penny, in for a pound. "When I faced the Kragzimik, you helped me," I answered, measuring each word. "You handed me the neutralizer."

"I had my reasons," she said, grabbing me by the

cheeks and slowly crushing my jaw. "I don't need to explain myself to you."

I shook my head and she released my face. I opened my mouth a few times to make sure my jaw was still intact.

"Monty's in trouble and I need to get him out of here."

"Tristan is on the third level, right-hand side, third door in," she said with a wave of her hand. "There, I helped you."

"I know all that," I lied. The location of his cell would make my finding him much easier. "I need you to remove this."

I held up my wrist and showed her the entropy stone bracelet that matched Peaches' collar.

"Entropy limiters." She smiled and I realized this might have been a bad idea. "The pain of removal will be excruciating."

"Ezra removed them without incident."

"I'm not Death, Splinter. I'm Karma, and here in this place, with me, *every* action has an equal and opposite reaction."

I gritted my teeth. "I'm beginning to think you just enjoy giving me pain."

"Life *is* pain," she said with a smile. "Your hellhound's collar too?"

"One condition," I said. "Whatever pain he was going to feel, you give it to me."

"You realize you're mortal right now?"

"Yes, I'm aware, but he shouldn't go through this pain because of my choice."

"Splinter, he's a hellhound. He can take more pain

than you can ever imagine, especially in this state. Are you certain?"

I nodded. "He gets no pain."

"This could kill you," she said quietly. "Is the mage worth it?"

"He's my family."

"This is going to be an eye-opener for you."

"What do you mean?" I asked. "My eyes are open."

"Not the one that counts."

"Then open it."

She nodded, placed both hands on either side of my face, and gave me a soft kiss on the forehead. It was unexpected and caught me by surprise. I was about to say something when my world exploded in pain.

She let me go and I fell to the floor, writhing in agony. Every cell of my body was on fire. The bones in my legs cracked first, followed by my arms. Muscles exploded, ligaments snapped, and tendons tore, shredded from the energy overload. Without my curse to mitigate the damage, my body was failing.

"Goodbye, Splinter," she said, shaking her head. "I do think this time you will die your last death. Enjoy the pain."

She disappeared and the flow of time snapped back to normal. I could hear Peaches whine as he stepped close to me. My body flushed hot, but it was a losing battle, the damage was catastrophic.

<I think I'm going to have to leave you, boy.>

He crawled next to me and placed his massive head under my hand.

<I will help you. This will hurt more. Prepare.>

"More?" I said with a gasp and a short laugh. The

pain made it impossible to focus on our silent communication. "Nothing can hurt more than what I— oh, hell."

The runes on the side of his body blazed with energy. Every muscle in my destroyed arm screamed with renewed pain as the energy flowed between us.

As the power coursing through my arm increased, my body felt like it was disintegrating. I wanted to let go, but the agony made it impossible to move. I ground my teeth against the pain as tears streamed down my cheeks.

"This…this is too much, boy. Let me go."

<Do not fight the bond. Just a little longer now.>

The runes along his flanks increased in intensity, blinding me. The force of the energy between us increased. I felt him place a giant paw on my chest as he grew. With a *thwump,* a blast of energy traveled through me and pushed me into the floor, cratering the concrete.

Heat flushed my body to deal with the damage. My vision began tunneling in, and I was just about to lose consciousness when a wet smack slobbered me across the face. He wasn't bus-sized, but he was easily five times his normal height.

<THIS IS NO TIME FOR A NAP, BONDMATE.>

<A nap? Are you insane? Karma nearly killed me and you almost finished what she started.>

<CORRECTION. I PREVENTED YOUR IMMINENT DEATH AND MY SALIVA HAS JUST ACCELERATED YOUR HEALING.>

He was right. I was feeling better by the second, but I wasn't going to admit it. I winced at the XL voice and shook my head.

<Lower the volume. My brain can't take your yelling right now.>

I got to my feet slowly as my body repaired itself. I noticed the entropy collar and bracelet were gone.

<THE DISRUPTION IN ENERGY HAS ATTRACTED THE ATTENTION OF THE SENTRIES.>

I turned to the doorway just in time to see the head of a Troll come into view. He pointed the flail in my direction.

"You two are trespassing." A huge smile crossed his face. "Guess I'm having hellhound for dinner."

TWENTY-FIVE

IT BECAME CLEAR in the first few seconds that this troll had never encountered a hellhound in battlemode.

The troll stepped into the room, swinging the flail on one side of his body. A sick grin crossed his face as he closed the distance. I focused and materialized Ebonsoul. The troll stopped advancing and examined my blade. He gave a short laugh and shook his head.

"You brought the wrong weapon," the troll said with a sneer. "I think I'll crush you first, then your tasty dog."

"My hellhound isn't on the menu."

I stepped in front of Peaches, which put me directly in the path of the troll. I kept an eye on the spiked balls as they swung in a lazy circle. The runes on the handle gave off a faint red glow every time he swung the flail.

"You plan on scratching me with your toy knife?" the troll asked. "I don't even sense magic from you."

"I don't need magic to deal with ugliness like you."

I totally needed magic to deal with a monster like him. Preferably one of Monty's nuclear solutions that erased everything.

The troll shook his head. "We have a name for confused people like you."

"Really?"

"Victim," the troll said and laughed. It was the equivalent of several broken fingernails pulled down the surface of a chalkboard. "Your weapon won't work on me. It's not a soul render."

"You're right, it's not." I glanced at Ebonsoul. "But I'm pretty sure it'll stab you just as well."

<PLEASE STEP TO ONE SIDE, BONDMATE.>

I moved away from Peaches as twin beams of energy shot from his eyes and punched through the troll's chest. He looked down at the large hole in the center of his body in shock.

"How did you—?" the troll managed before falling backward. A few seconds later, he was a mound of dust.

I looked at Peaches, as surprised as the troll.

<*How did you do that?*>

<DO WHAT?>

<*What do you mean do what? You blasted that troll to dust.*>

<YES. HE WAS AN IMMINENT AND PRESENT THREAT. HE NEEDED TO BE NEUTRALIZED BEFORE HE HARMED YOU.>

<*I thought magic was inhibited in Sheol?*>

<IF YOU LEAVE THIS ROOM, THE CURSE THAT KEEPS YOU ALIVE WOULD BE GREATLY DIMINISHED, YES.>

<*So your magic eye-beams only work in this room?*>

<I NEVER SAID *MY* ABILITIES WOULD BE

DIMINISHED. I AM NOT MAGIC.>

<Excuse me? I think I missed something there.>

<HAVE YOUR AUDITORY SENSES SUFFERED DAMAGE?>

He stepped close with his tongue hanging out. I put my hands up quickly.

<My ears are fine. What do you mean you're not magic? Have you seen what you can do?>

<I AM COGNIZANT OF MY ABILITIES.>

<You're telling me you don't use magic to blink out, grow to XL size or fire omega beams and roast trolls?>

< I CAST NO RUNES NOR UTTER ANY SPELLS.>

He was right. He did everything without having to trace runes, not that he could.

<Then how?>

<I AM A HELLHOUND.>

<Right, that answers everything.>

<IT USUALLY DOES.>

<I know where Monty is. Can you deal with the Trolls?>

<YES. YOU MUST REMOVE THE MAGE FROM THIS LOCATION WITH HASTE. THE MAGICAL PROPERTIES OF THIS LOCATION ARE PLACING HIS LIFE IN DANGER.>

<Third level, third door on right side. Let's go.>

We ran out of the room and I felt the energy crawl over my skin like angry ants. The Pit was a self-contained space of magic-inhibiting defenses. The enso pendant around my neck felt warm and gave off a soft glow as we headed to the nearest ramp.

A shift in the energy around us made me pause.

<What was that?>

<THIS LOCATION HAS COMMENCED AN INTERPHASIC TRANSMUTATION. IT WILL BE NON-EXISTENT SHORTLY.>

<English. The kind I can understand.>

<MY APOLOGIES. THE AREA KNOWN AS THE PIT IS SHIFTING THROUGH PLANES. IT APPEARS TO DO THIS IN SECTIONS. IT HAS BEGUN WITH THE LOWEST LEVEL.>

<What's under the lowest level?>

<NOTHING.>

I looked over the edge of the platform and counted only four levels. The fifth level was disappearing. The advancing darkness slowly swallowed the platform. The troll that patrolled that level had climbed the ramp and now walked the fourth.

"Shit. We need to get to Monty"—a vise-like pressure squeezed my body and released me a moment later —"now."

<PLEASE MOVE WITH HASTE. WE ARE RUNNING OUT OF TIME.>

We were on the third level. I ran to the third door and fired Grim Whisper. Nothing happened. Above us, I could hear the trolls advancing. I guess they didn't mind making noise when attacking trespassers.

<We have about ten seconds before those trolls try to introduce us to their pointy balls of pain.>

<THE WEAPONS THEY ARE CURRENTLY WIELDING ARE DESIGNATED AS RUNIC FLAILS, NOT POINTY BALLS OF PAIN.>

Professor Peaches was getting on my last nerve. I was about to comment, but I remembered this was his normal method of speech. I just couldn't understand him when he was smaller. He was actually simplifying his speech pattern so I would comprehend him. I shook my head at the thought.

<Fine. Can you open this door?>

<I CANNOT. DUCK.>

<No need to resort to name-calling. Just because you can't——>

Peaches stepped forward and shoved me with his enormous head. I flew forward three feet, landed on my stomach, and slid for another three feet before coming to a stop. Several of the flail spheres were embedded in the wall where I'd stood moments earlier.

Peaches turned and fired his omega beams across the platform, blasting another troll to dust. I looked over the edge and noticed half of the fourth level was gone.

<Can you read the runes on the door? Maybe there's a clue to opening it.>

Peaches went to the door and examined the runes. He wasn't magic, but I figured he was versed in runes and a genius in this state.

<CAUSE AND EFFECT—IN THIS PLACE EVERY ACTION HAS AN EQUAL AND OPPOSITE REACTION. TO GAIN ACCESS, SET YOUR LIFE ABLAZE.>

<What does that mean?>

<I BELIEVE THIS IS COMMONLY KNOWN AS GIBBERISH.>

<No. Karma said something similar to me earlier.>

<YOU SPOKE TO THE ELEMENT OF CAUSALITY?>

<Yes, she was the one who removed your collar. Well, technically it was me, but she helped.>

<IT'S CLEAR YOU HAVE SUFFERED BRAIN

TRAUMA. ALLOW ME TO SALIVATE UPON YOU. MY SALIVA HAS HEALING PROPERTIES.>

I pushed him away before he could give me a slobber bath turning the statement over in my head.

<*Don't lick me, my brain has always been damaged. Those runes have to be the key.*>

<THESE DOORS HAVE NO LOCKS AND THEREFORE DO NOT REQUIRE KEYS. WOULD YOU LIKE ME TO BLAST YOU WITH MY BEAMS? I'M CERTAIN THAT WOULD SET YOUR LIFE AND MOST OF YOUR BODY ABLAZE.>

<*Thanks, but no, I don't think that's what it means. You said my curse is limited here, but do I have access to some of the magic?*>

<YES. MOVE BACK.>

Another troll advanced as Peaches blinked out, leaving me standing several feet away from an angry approaching troll who leaped at me. I raised Ebonsoul as Peaches blinked back in behind it and rammed the troll mid-jump over the platform edge and into the abyss.

<*A little warning next time would be nice.*>

<I ADVISED YOU TO MOVE BACK. THAT IS A LITTLE WARNING.>

I absorbed Ebonsoul and ran to Monty's door. I had an idea. If it didn't work we were going to find out if this abyss was really bottomless. The darkness crept up the ramp from the mostly gone fourth level.

"*Ignisvitae,*" I said under my breath. The violet orb that formed in my palm was small, only about three inches across, but the energy it contained was overwhelming. I had to avert my gaze to avoid being blinded.

I extended my arm and pushed the orb at the door. It blasted forward faster than I could track, slamming into the metal and splashing across its surface.

The red runes pulsed with energy for a second before disappearing, along with the door. I ran in and saw a semi-conscious Monty lying on the floor. He turned his head in my direction when he heard me enter, but his reaction was off somehow.

"Quite vivid," Monty slurred. "It's good to see you again, Simon. Even if it's only in my imagination."

"Peaches! I need you here now."

<ONE MOMENT. I AM ELIMINATING THREATS.>

I turned Monty over slowly. Only a small piece of the shattered bloody bloom remained on his jacket. His face was swollen in several places and dried blood covered one side of his face.

I couldn't sense his energy signature, but I figured that had more to do with the Pit and the inhibiting runes around us. I removed the enso pendant I wore and placed it around his neck.

I propped up his head, pulled out my skull-covered flask and made him drink more than was probably safe. I heard the firing of Peaches' omega beams several more times before his silhouette filled the doorway.

<We need to get out of here. Now.>

< TRANSPORTING MORE THAN ONE PERSON AFTER CONSIDERABLE ENERGY EXPENDITURE WILL MAKE THIS DIFFICULT.>

<Difficult doesn't mean impossible. If we wait any longer, we get to disappear along with the Pit.>

<THIS FORM HAS TAXED MY ENERGY RESERVES. I WILL NEED REST AND SUSTENANCE PROVIDED THIS JUMP IS SUCCESSFUL.>

<*We need to get to the Randy Rump. You remember the werebear, Jimmy?*>

<I DO. PLEASE, HOLD ON.>

I grabbed Monty, slowly lifted him to his feet, and leaned him against Peaches' massive frame. I wrapped my other arm around Peaches' neck. The darkness had started devouring the third level.

<*Any time you're ready, boy.*>

The darkness had entered the room, and Peaches rumbled.

<PREPARE. I WILL USE THE ENCROACHING INTERPHASIC SHIFT TO PROPEL US.>

<*I must have misheard. That sounded like you're going to wait until the darkness envelops the level before getting out of here?*>

<PRECISELY.>

"Bloody hell," I said, wrapping my arm around Peaches' neck even tighter. The floor disappeared, everything went black, and we fell.

TWENTY-SIX

WE CRASHED THROUGH the Randy Rump's main window and stopped at the display case holding cold cuts. Several patrons scattered as we shattered a few tables on our way through the shop.

Jimmy the butcher leaped over the display case in one smooth movement, ready to pounce and attack. When he saw it was us, he went from insta-shred to damage control.

I looked up, disoriented, and heard Jimmy giving orders.

"Clear the back room," he said. "No, my office, now."

Several of the new employees picked up Monty and the normal-sized Peaches and removed them from the main floor.

"You look like hell," Jimmy said as he helped me to my feet. "I have instructions for you from your friends."

"It's been a rough day," I said, looking around at the crowded main area. "Why is this place so crowded?"

The Randy Rump was a block away from the Moscow and stayed open all night, only closing for a few hours in the early morning. It catered to the early evening and nighttime clientele—which was most of the supernatural community.

The Rump had also become a popular meeting place since the Dark Council had declared its neutral status. It had gone from "butcher shop" to "butcher shop, restaurant, and meeting hall" in a few short weeks. But even with its changed status and growing clientele, I had never seen it so crowded.

"Should I have made a reservation?" I asked. My head throbbed from our landing, but I felt my body flush warm, taking care of the damage.

"To crash through my window?" Jimmy asked. "No, you, Tristan and Peaches are always welcome. I just wish you'd use the door occasionally. I just had that window redone."

"What's with the added security? Did someone try casting in here?"

I counted ten mage guards standing or sitting in strategic locations throughout the seating area. They had calmed down once they saw Jimmy speaking to me.

By nightfall, the mage guards would be replaced with vampires or shifters of some sort. The Dark Council took the safety and neutrality of its designated locations seriously. Violating the established rules of neutral locations could end in permanent retirement…from life.

"The streets haven't been safe these past few days," Jimmy answered, following my gaze around the shop. "Revenants are roaming the streets and it's getting worse every day. Every neutral zone is like this."

"The Council is taking this threat seriously?"

Jimmy nodded and led me to his office. "The attacks are against all of us. Last night we lost two mages. Night before that, a group of vampires."

"NYTF?" I asked. "Ramirez?"

Jimmy shook his head. "This is way above their pay grade. They stopped going on patrol after an entire squad was eaten."

"Eaten?"

"And turned on the spot," he replied. "One moment NYTF officers, next moment, revenants."

"Damn," I said. "This is bad."

"I don't want to jump to any conclusions," Jimmy said, glancing at me, "but are you and Tristan involved in this somehow?"

He opened the office door. and I waited until he closed and secured the office before I brought him up to speed.

A large desk sat against the far wall, opposite the door. To the right of the desk and along the wall sat a large brown sofa. On the other side of the desk, against the left wall, I saw two tall, black filing cabinets.

His desk was neat, with several piles of papers in organized stacks along the surface. An industrial-sized computer monitor took up almost half the desk.

Even though the office was spacious, it still felt slightly cramped because Jimmy was just this side of enormous. I wondered if all werebears were his size since I'd never seen him in his animal shape. He was the only werebear I knew.

I waited until he closed and secured the office before

I brought him up to speed. He sat in the chair behind the desk and leaned forward resting his elbows. The chair creaked and screamed for mercy under his huge frame.

"Do you need help?" he asked, handing me an envelope. "I can leave the shop to the Council and assist with this."

I shook my head. "No, you need to be here. Your presence helps keep this neutral zone in place."

"Except when you guys visit," he said with a tight smile. "It's almost as if your group is cursed."

I winced. "I'll make sure we take care of the damage," I said. "Can you make sure Peaches gets fed? Where's Monty?"

"I'll bring the hellhound his bowl. Tristan and Peaches are in the backroom. Through there."

He pointed to the door in rear of the office.

The door was a smaller version of the main door in the butcher shop, securing the entrance to the backroom. The door and frame were made of Australian Buloke ironwood.

I narrowed my eyes and saw that Jimmy had added to the runes since our last visit. Magical inscriptions covered every inch of its surface. It stood six feet tall and half as wide. I was sure Jimmy had to stoop to get in that way.

"Those are new," I said, pointing to the door. "Is that an erasure rune?"

He nodded and approached the door, pressing the runes in sequence. He pulled on the handle, which looked tiny in his massive hand.

"Thought it was a good idea after the Negomancer."

The door was over a foot thick. Opening it was surprisingly easy if you knew the rune sequence. If you didn't, you'd need the equivalent of a magical nuke, and that would probably just scratch the surface. Once closed, it remained closed. Period.

It swung open easily and I looked inside. The backroom of the Rump was smaller than the front area. It usually consisted of one large room with three tables. It now served as a kind of triage space. The tables were gone and I saw people moving around, tending to the wounded.

Jimmy had added several rows of beds. I saw a few of them were actual hospital beds complete with crash carts next to them. Monty lay in one of these beds. The Randy Rump had become a mini-Haven.

No one approached Monty's bed. It probably had something to do with the hellhound sporting softly glowing runes across his flank while snoring at his feet, but I could have been mistaken.

"I had one of my people call Haven," Jimmy said as we stepped over to Monty's bed. "Roxanne will be here soon."

"Thanks, Jimmy. I really appreciate this."

"You can thank me by not blowing up the Rump," he said with a smile. "I need to get back outside and calm down the trigger-happy mages out there. You good?"

I nodded. "I think we're okay for now," I said, holding up the envelope. "I need to read this, and see how Monty is doing."

Jimmy nodded and headed for the smaller door. He stopped and turned before leaving the backroom. I walked over to where he stood.

"His energy signature is different somehow," Jimmy said in a low voice. "Is he okay?"

I looked over at Monty. "Mageopause, I think," I answered. "I'm a detective, not a doctor, Jim. I'm sure Roxanne will know more."

Jimmy stared at me for a second and shook his head. "Mageopause, really?" he said as he ducked, stepping through the door and back into his office. "Whatever it is, it may be safer to keep him here. Let Roxanne know."

"I'll tell her. Thanks again," I said as he closed the door.

A portal opened next to me and Roxanne stepped through with a small cadre of nurses and security personnel.

"Simon," she said with a curt nod and raised a hand "Give me a second." She turned to her people and gave them instructions. I saw the security detail fan out around the back room and the nurses move to Monty's bed.

"Tell me what happened," she said, approaching Monty.

I told her everything that had occurred since I'd last seen her. She listened in silence until we reached Monty's side.

"What happened to the bloom?" she said, lifting the enso pendant and letting it fall gently on his chest. She removed the remaining pieces of the bloom and put them in her pocket.

"I don't know. It was like that when I found him."

"Where were you?" she asked, her voice suddenly hard. "You're his shieldbearer."

"Doing what needed to be done," Monty said hoarsely. "He found me in the Pit."

Roxanne turned to face me. For a brief second I thought she was going to blast me across the room. She took a deep breath and exhaled, regaining her composure.

"The Pit?" She looked at Monty. "Are you referring to Sheol?"

Monty nodded. "I don't know how you found me. No one knows where Sheol is, much less the Pit."

"Technically it was LD who helped me find you. He knows a guy."

"Division 13?" Monty asked. "The Ten never cease to amaze."

"Yes, oh shit," I said, remembering. "I left the Dark Goat near the Hell Gate Bridge."

"I'll call Cecil and have him put retrieval runes on it," Monty answered, getting out of bed. "We can't have that vehicle sitting around the city. It's liable to cause massive destruction."

"The *vehicle* is going to cause massive destruction?" I said incredulously. "Really?"

"We need to stop William." Monty removed the enso pendant and handed it back. "Thank you, it helped."

Roxanne crossed her arms and blocked him. "You're in no condition to stop anyone."

"Gabrielle dropped me off to remove the threat I posed," he said. "Apparently, William is controlling her and Niall."

"You said his name."

"I know," Monty said. "I want them to know I'm coming."

"William is after the lost runes," I said. "I don't think he's after the source of magic. I think he wants to *become* a source of magic."

"Impossible," Roxanne said. "No one mage is powerful enough to wield all five stones even if they managed to find them."

"The Black Heart is the lynchpin," Monty said, gently moving Roxanne to one side. "If he obtains it he can locate the other four."

"Three," I corrected. "He has the White Heart."

"Where was it?"

"Shamballa. I think we helped him escape his confinement."

"Is the Abbott alive?" Monty asked and grabbed Roxanne's hand. "I must do this."

"You haven't completed your shift," Roxanne answered. "He'll kill you."

"I have my shieldbearer and his hellhound," he said, looking at me. "I'll be safe."

Roxanne glanced at me. "His past performance doesn't inspire much confidence. At least stay until your shift is complete."

"William has the White Heart. He'll try for the Black next. I can't."

"You mean you *won't.*"

"I mean he's my brother and I must stop him before he tries to join all the lost runes and destroys himself," Monty said. "If he tries to combine the two, and make the Gray Heart without the proper sequence, he'll kill himself."

"Let him," Roxanne said, her voice hard. "He was going to let you rot in the Pit. If Simon hadn't found you—"

"I'd be dead by now, I know," Monty answered. "I'm not William. My shift is complete, look for yourself."

Roxanne stood back and narrowed her eyes. After a few seconds, she flexed her jaw and dropped her arms.

"How?" she asked after a moment of silence. "I don't see traces of the neutralizing."

"Being dropped in a magical null zone during a neutralized shift seems to accelerate the shifting process," Monty said. "I promise to be safe."

"You're a man of action, lies do not become you." Roxanne smoothed out his jacket. "You'll be safe right up to the moment you leave this place."

"If not safe, then careful."

"That, I can believe. Go stop him, then. Afterwards, we need to speak."

"About?"

"Us."

Roxanne placed a hand on his cheek and stepped away, moving to examine the rest of the patients in the room. I heard her slip into doctor-mode and give instructions to the nearby nurses.

"That sounded serious," I said once she was out of earshot. "Usually when a woman says we need to speak, something is wrong."

"Nothing is wrong," Monty said, following Roxanne with his gaze. "She wants an assurance I won't—can't—give her."

"Does she know why?"

"No, and I can't tell her that either."

"Sounds like it's going to be a *conversation*. I suggest having it in a neutral location."

"We'll burn that bridge when we get to it."

"Did you just Dex me?" I asked. "Really?"

"The Abbott," Monty said, waving my words away. "Was he still alive when you left Shamballa?"

I nodded. "At first I thought he was part of William's plan. Now I think he's just doing some Zen thing and letting matters run their course."

"Zhuchi is a chronomancer," Monty said as if that explained anything.

"He can magically tell time?" I asked. "I don't need magic for that, just a watch."

"Zhuchi is also Master Yat's teacher."

"Well, that explains a few things. What's a chronomaster?"

"Chronomancer," Monty corrected. "He can shape time and see the possible outcomes."

"Fighting him must be pure joy," I said. "Do you think he allowed William to take the White Heart because he saw it as the best of the possible outcomes?"

"Possibly," Monty said, looking at me. "Have you suffered a head injury recently?"

"No, why do you ask?"

"You sound more lucid than usual," Monty answered. "Are you certain?"

"Getting you out of the Pit wasn't a picnic, if you're asking," I said, looking at the snoring hellhound still snuggled comfortably on the bed. "Peaches went on troll-trouncing duty."

"He is truly a fearsome creature."

"And starving too," I added. "You're going to have to make him large quantities of meat."

I nudged Peaches gently and rolled him off the bed. He fell with a thud and shook the bed.

<Was that necessary?>

<No, but it was definitely satisfying.>

<Next time I need to bite you, I'm going to do it hard.>

<This is no time for a nap. We have to go.>

<We just got here. This is the perfect time for a nap. Do you have meat?>

<We'll get some on the way. Come on.>

Peaches padded over to me, shook his entire body, and proceeded to give Monty an extra dose of hungry puppy eyes and bared his teeth. All of nurses moved away from our side of the room.

<You know that look doesn't really work, especially when your eyes glow red and you look menacing.>

<I do not look menacing. I look hungry.>

Monty glanced at Peaches and then looked back at me. "Thank you," he said. "Any longer in there and I'd probably be erased by now, or worse."

"You would have done the same for me," I said, waving his words away. "I wasn't going to leave you in there."

<Ask him if he can make me some meat. Not the undead kind, please.>

Monty nodded. "I would have certainly extricated you from there had you been captured," he said. "I know I wasn't acting normally."

"You were being a ginormous ass," I said. "I was almost tempted to leave your megalomaniacal mageness in there."

"Thank you for resisting," Monty said with a nod. "Is your creature in need of food right now? He keeps giving me those eyes."

<I told you it worked. Yes, please.>

<Don't get used to this.>

"Make it to go. We need to look at this"—I held up the envelope—"and go find LD and TK."

Monty gestured and formed a long group of linked sausage. Peaches pounced on it and began devouring.

"Do you think you can reason with William?" I said while admiring the velocity of hellhound sausage suction. "Maybe you can convince him to go on a prolonged vacation on a different plane for one or two millennia."

"My brother and I have a difficult relationship," Monty said as we headed to the door that led back to Jimmy's office. "He and I have never seen eye to eye on most things. If I can speak to him, we may be able to come to some kind of compromise."

"Oh, like he wants to become a god and wield world-ending magic and you should die? That kind of compromise?"

"Preferably one that's less fatal," Monty answered, looking back at Roxanne. She glanced his way, put two fingers to her heart, and then her forehead. Monty returned the gesture.

"What did that mean?" I asked, curious. "Two hearts, one brain? Is she the one with the brain?"

"It means always in my heart and thoughts," he answered with a sigh. "It's the first part of a sorcerer curse designed to explode an enemy's heart and kill from a distance."

I stared at him for a second. "You two *really* need to have a conversation."

"Says the man marked by an ancient vampire."

"That's different," I answered. "We have an understanding."

"You understand that she has claimed you for herself," Monty said with a nod. "They say acceptance is the first step to recovery. In this case, you may recover your freedom."

"That's not what I meant."

Monty pressed the rune sequence, pausing for a moment at the new erasure addition. "An erasure rune? It would seem James is taking security seriously."

"Probably our fault," I said, following Monty into the office. "We—and by we I mean *you*—have helped renovate the Rump a few times."

"A valid point," Monty said, closing the door behind us and locking it. "More security is always a wise precaution in a neutral location."

"Especially one so close to where we live," I added. "LD said to stay in the Rump. Shouldn't we wait?"

Monty extended a hand. "Let's see what the message from them says."

"How do you know it's from them?"

Monty waved a hand over the envelope and a large black and golden X appeared on one side. "I'd say this is a solid clue."

"That's a neat trick," I said, watching the X slowly disappear. "What did he do, write a note in lemon juice?"

Monty formed an orb of fire and dropped it on the paper. Runes appeared on one side. I couldn't make them out, but I saw Monty's expression harden.

"Fordey is compromised, but they managed to get

the Black Heart out in time. LD wants us to meet them."

"What?" I said, surprised. "Where?"

"They're in the Fordey Vault." Monty pinched his nose. "Which means this will be bloody difficult if it's locked down."

"How do we get in?"

"We need to go see Aria again," he said. "Did you manage to keep the books she gave me?"

"TK has them. Yat made sure she kept them."

Monty nodded. "Just as well. If I know TK, she'll have read them by now."

"Hellfire?" I asked, not looking forward to another trip to the club. "Maybe Erik can meet us somewhere?"

"No, I can open a portal to the Wordweavers from here."

Monty gestured. Violet runes floated from his fingers and slowly vanished into the air. A second later, a portal formed. It revealed a large office on the other side.

"Let's do this," I said, approaching the portal. "Anything is better than a teleportation circle."

Monty nodded. "By the way, mageopause is not a real condition."

TWENTY-SEVEN

WE STEPPED INTO a spacious office. Immediately we were surrounded by several wordweavers.

"Stand down," Aria said as the wordweavers spread out. "Leave us."

The wordweavers looked uncertainly at Aria, who nodded. The air around us crackled with energy as they filed out of the office.

Aria's office reminded me of Erik's office in the Hellfire. Shelves of books lined almost every wall. A large oak desk dominated one side of the space, while a long worktable covered with beakers and open texts sat against the only wall not bristling with shelves weighed down by books.

"Erik would never open a portal into my office," Aria said and narrowed her eyes at Monty. "The only explanation is you've shifted."

"I apologize for the intrusion," Monty said. "But we're pressed for time."

"William found the White Heart." It wasn't a question. She sat behind her desk, steepled her fingers, and pressed them against her lips.

"You knew?" Monty asked. "This is what you had Yat doing?"

"I had information that William was searching for the lost runes," she said. "I knew the Black Heart was secure in Fordey. Is it still secure in Fordey?"

"It's been moved to the vault," Monty said and gave her the letter. "We need to gain entrance."

"If William gets the Black Heart, he will try to form the Gray Heart," Aria said.

"He doesn't have the sequence," Monty said. "It will kill him, destroy the vault, and unleash enough residual energy to reduce the city to a magical wasteland."

"City? Which city?"

"The Fordey Vault is more than ten stories beneath Grand Central Station," Monty said. "That would be the Grand Central Station in *our* city."

"It is the greatest good to the greatest number of people, which is the measure of right and wrong," Aria said quietly. "I'm sorry."

"The needs of the many outweigh the needs of the few?" Monty asked. "You would sacrifice an entire city?"

"The city has over eight million people," I said. "You would let them die?"

"The planet has over seven billion. Would you risk them all?" She rested both palms on her desk. "I can't help you. The danger is too great."

"Is she refusing to help us?" I asked, looking at Monty. "I don't understand. Did she just Spock us?"

"No, she wants William to activate the Black Heart. It will destroy him and vaporize the city."

I turned on Aria. "Are you insane?" I yelled. "We need to stop him."

She stared at me and my brain realized I had just lost it with possibly one of the most powerful mages on the planet. Didn't mean she wasn't a shit, it just meant she was a shit with enough power to blow me to bits with a word.

"The sequence," Monty said, his voice cutting through the air. I felt his energy signature increase. "You gave him the wrong sequence?"

"No, I gave him the right sequence," she said. "I just gave him the wrong trigger."

"Monty," I said slowly as his energy signature kept increasing. He may have shifted, but I didn't think he was anywhere near Aria's weight class yet. "There has to be another way."

"Heed your shieldbearer, mage," she said. "This die has been cast. The Wordweavers will not move to help you."

"They're not going to help," I said. "Let's go. We're wasting time."

"It also means they will not move to hinder us," Monty answered, staring at Aria. "Correct?"

Aria flexed her jaw and sat a bit more rigid as she stared back at Monty. "Correct, Tristan," she said. "Tread carefully, you walk a sword's edge. You should take care not to cut yourself with your own arrogance. This is a mistake."

"What you call arrogance, I call certainty." He gestured, opening a portal. On the other side, I could see 42nd Street and Grand Central. "Only those who do nothing make no mistakes."

We stepped through the portal and left Aria behind. Nighttime on 42nd Street meant crowds. Except tonight. I looked around the entrance to Grand Central opposite Pershing Square. Not one person was on the street.

"I know the city's been a bit wary of revenants, but I've never seen 42nd deserted like this."

Monty paused for a moment and closed his eyes. "Gabrielle," he said, raising his hand to deflect a black orb of energy. "That won't work."

I drew Grim Whisper and turned to face a handful of revenants approaching us from across the street.

"She must be tired, I count about five or six of them," I said, taking aim. "We can clear this fast."

Monty tapped me on the shoulder. "Those are undead mages. Her main force is over there."

I looked west and saw several hundred revenants closing on us. "What the hell? Change of plans," I said, pulling the door to Grand Central open. "We avoid the dead people and stop William."

"Good plan," Monty said, unleashing a fireball into the mob as he followed me. "We need to get to the lower level. The entrance to the vault is near the trains."

We ran down the wide ramps with the sound of revenants behind us. The undead mages moved faster than the regular revenants.

"Did she turn all the people on 42nd street?" I asked as we turned the corner and ran down another ramp. We arrived on the lowest level and I saw Monty checking track numbers. "Which track?"

"Track 13, find it."

"They're all triple digits down here. Are you sure it's

not on the upper level?"

"Track 13 is on this level."

The sound of the revenants was getting closer. Monty gestured and pushed his hands at the sound of revenants. I felt a wave of energy rush along the floor and crash into the undead mages. They launched into the air and fell in every direction. It slowed them down but didn't stop the onslaught.

"This is a George Romero nightmare," I said, moving to the opposite side of the level. "Can you freeze them?"

"Not enough water nearby," Monty said and traced more runes in the air. "We need to get off this level."

I narrowed my eyes and saw a non-descript door at the end of a small corridor. A small ticket counter partially blocked the corridor from view.

"Monty, over here," I said, my voice reverberating through the level. A sign read to Track 13. I grabbed the handle to pull the door open.

"Simon, wait!" Monty yelled as he approached. "Do not pull the handle."

He gestured and I saw the runes etched into the door and floor. All around the small corridor runes pulsed with energy.

"Can I let go?" I said as Peaches whined next to me. "Or will it set off an explosion?"

"If you let go now, this whole corridor collapses on us," he said, tracing the runes along the floor and leading away from the door. "Give me a moment."

"Sure, we only have the walking dead headed this way to munch on us. Take your time."

He read more of the runes and nodded his head.

"When I tell you, push the door forward."

"But the handle makes it seem…Oh, got it."

He formed a golden lattice and covered the entrance to the small corridor. With another gesture, a set of golden runes flowed across the floor and into the door.

"Now, Simon. Push."

I shoved the handle forward and felt a rush of energy race up my arm as the door opened inward. I stumbled forward and Monty grabbed me by the shoulder, stopping me from going over the edge of a small platform and landing on a station about fifty feet below us.

A one-car train sat at the station waiting for passengers that would never arrive. Its rectangular shape was squat and gray, reminding me of the current subway that ran under and around the city. I saw a large "13" on the wall opposite the train.

"That would've hurt," I said, looking down.

"I'm pretty sure that was the intention. We need to get down to that train."

We ran down the stairs and arrived at the bottom, when the fear gripped me.

"Hello, Tristan." I recognized the voice and wished I didn't. "I've been waiting for you. William promised me you would come."

Monty and I stood still on the last landing. Even Peaches remained silent. I looked around and realized why. Shadowforms filled the station, blocking our path to the train.

"Niall, William is only using you," Monty said. "Once he gets the lost runes, he'll discard you—or worse, erase you."

"He said you'd say that. He saved me from the Elders and _you_." Niall pointed at Monty. "You all wanted me dead. William saved me. Saved me because I'm special, unique."

"And slightly deranged," I said to Monty under my breath. "He's not all there."

"Pavormancers have short life spans, because the discipline eats away at their mental capacities," Monty replied in a low voice. "It's why I initially recommended erasure."

"I'm going to kill you now. You're going to experience your greatest fear over and over until you beg me to kill you."

"That sounds fun," I said, firing Grim Whisper. The bullets missed and I knew he had pulled his little portal trick. "Is that really you or are you _scared_ to come face us?"

"Simon?" Monty asked. "You've never faced a Pavormancer."

"No, but I've faced worse. I've been up close and personal with the greatest bitch in existence," I answered and stepped off the landing into the station. "Come on out!"

Niall stepped onto the station opposite me. I knew it was him and not a shadow because the wave of fear that hit me threatened to drive me insane. In a split second, I experienced every worst-case scenario I could imagine. When it was over, I gasped, trying to catch my breath.

"You don't look so good, Simon," Niall said with a laugh. "What's the matter? Are you scared?"

I remembered the Void passage, dealing with Karma,

facing a Fomor and staring the Morrigan in the face.

"No," I said once I gathered my breath. "Fear isn't real. Danger is real, but fear is a choice."

"So eloquent," Niall said and gestured. "I'll make sure to remember that as you claw your eyes out and end your pitiful existence."

Another wave of fear flooded the station. I glanced to the side and saw Monty on his knees, trying to fend off the energy washing over us. Peaches was trying to chomp on the shadowforms and failing. It was like trying to grab smoke.

The anger rose in my chest. It was a small flame at first. I focused and took a step toward Niall. The shadowforms clawed at my legs and arms. I heard Niall's laughter as they swarmed me.

I let the anger grow into a blaze and then materialized Ebonsoul. I ran at Niall as he unleashed more black fear. Behind me, I heard Monty scream. Niall tried to back away but I was too fast, too unexpected. No one had withstood his fearcasting before.

I plunged Ebonsoul into his chest and it began to siphon his energy. I wanted nothing of it. It felt tainted, laced with darkness, frustration, sadness, and fear.

"*Ignisvitae*," I said and let the energy flow through Ebonsoul. For the first time, a Pavormancer felt authentic fear—his own. "You don't fuck with my family."

I pushed Ebonsoul deeper and unleashed all the power I held. A violet orb of energy raced from my hand into the blade and erupted inside Niall. He stepped back, clawing at his chest. The shadowforms stopped attacking me and raced back to him, but it was too late. An explosion of violet energy catapulted me into the stairs. I landed hard with the breath knocked out of me.

A wet towel smacked me across the face. "What the hell?" I said, looking up, realizing the "towel" was a large hellhound tongue. "Stop with the bath."

<My saliva is good for you.>

<Why didn't you bite him? He tried to melt my brain.>

<He smelled bad. I don't want to taste bad things.>

<And it's okay if he melts my brain?>

<Yes, you said you don't use it too much.>

I shook my head and made my way over to Monty, who was slowly getting to his feet.

"How did you withstand his onslaught?" he asked. "It was all I could do to remain ahead of his fearcasting. I almost succumbed near the end."

"Pavormancy really sucks," I said, "but I've learned fear doesn't exist. It's an idea in someone's head. That's why it's different for everyone."

"That doesn't explain how you withstood his attack."

I looked down at the enso pendant hanging from my chest. It was giving off a soft glow.

"Maybe it has something to do with this." I held up the glowing pendant. "Could be I'm stronger as a shieldbearer."

"Possible but improbable."

"What now?"

"William isn't here," Monty said, looking around. "He must be at the vault."

"The vault? I thought this was the vault?"

"No, this is how we get there." Monty pointed to the

train. "We need to go down to the Fordey Vault."

"Down? How far down?"

"The Ten appropriated the old M42 basement and converted it into a vault for items too dangerous to keep in the boutique," Monty said. "When that became full, they took that space, expanded it, and created a secure lower level about a hundred feet below the original basement."

"Can William get in there?"

"Normally I would say no," Monty said, stepping onto the train. I followed him, and Peaches got on next to me, making the car sway slightly. "Only the Ten have access to the lower vault, but these are extenuating circumstances."

"He has the White Heart," I said. "That changes everything. Still think you can reason with him?"

Monty gestured and pressed a hand on a panel. The panel lit up and I felt the train lurch forward.

"He's my brother," Monty said after a moment. "I'm going to try."

"And if he doesn't listen?"

"Then I'll perform an erasure on him."

"Somehow, I don't think he's going to sit still for that," I said. "The White Heart is *inside* him, so an erasure may not work."

"The Gray Heart can't be formed. He has the wrong trigger. It will destroy him."

"He won't believe you," I said slowly. "If he's come this far, nothing is going to stop him."

"If he won't listen to reason, I'll stop him— permanently."

TWENTY-EIGHT

<WE CAN'T let Monty kill his brother.>

<Why would he want to kill his brother?>

<His brother wants to do something bad that will hurt many people. He won't listen to Monty.>

<Do you want me to bite his brother? I could bite him and stop him.>

<No—well, yes. Can you find Dex?>

<The Birdman who makes good meat?>

<Yes. Can you locate him even from down here?>

<Yes. His scent is very strong. I can find him anywhere.>

<Good. I'm going to give you a signal. When I do, this is what I want you to do.>

I broke down the plan to save Monty. If I let Monty kill William, I had a bad feeling the experience would transform him. No matter how evil William was, I couldn't let Monty kill him.

After what seemed like forever, the train began to slow. It pulled into a station similar to the one under Grand Central. Monty and I got off and looked around.

This station was twice the size of the one near Grand

Central. It was mostly marble embedded into the schist that formed the bedrock of the city.

One corridor led away from the station. We took it and ended up in a large antechamber. Symbols and designs decorated the walls around us. The ones I could decipher were created to contain and inhibit. I let my senses expand and realized all the runes in this room were dormant.

This must have been the original M42 basement, before the Ten expanded the Fordey Vault and moved the artifacts and items lower.

"This is the original vault, isn't it?" I asked.

Monty nodded. "The new vault is below us," he said. "I was certain he'd be here."

"Maybe he just gave it up," I said, examining the area. "I mean, even if he got the Black Heart he still has to find the other three."

"True," Monty said. "Unless Yat knows the location of those as well. Then it's just a matter of getting the Black Heart and forming the Gray."

A beam of white energy punched Monty into a nearby wall.

"I gave that stupid cow one simple task," William said, materializing across from us. Both his hands shone with white energy. "All she had to do was make sure you were trapped in the Pit."

"That would have killed Monty."

"That was the idea," William said, taking aim and sending a blast of energy my way. I barely deflected his blast as I pressed my mala bead and formed my shield.

"He's your brother, doesn't that mean anything?"

"Of course, he's my family," William said, forming

several orbs in his hands. "It means he dies first."

"There's a big difference between being related and being family."

I ran over to Monty, shield first. William unleashed a barrage of orbs that slammed me into the wall. I managed to deflect most of them, but my arm took a pounding.

"Killing him won't get you into the vault," I said between gasps. My arm felt like tenderized meat. "This is futile."

"Wrong. Killing him serves one of my main objectives," William said, absorbing the orbs and forming a long dark blade in his hand. "Once I eliminate my little brother, they'll come out to investigate, practically inviting me inside."

His response told me everything I needed to know. He may have had the White Heart, but he didn't possess the power to force himself into the Fordey Vault. He needed them to open it from the inside. I needed him to lose control.

"That's never going to happen," I countered. "They know better than to let you in."

"You'd be surprised how foolish people can be when lives are at stake," William said, firing another blast and cratering the wall next to me. "They act against their best interests. I've seen it countless times. Take you, for example."

"Me?"

William nodded. "Here you are, trying to save my brother," he said. "That is an exercise in futility. The inevitability of your deaths has been determined. You're only prolonging what will occur. If you had run and saved yourself, you wouldn't be here facing me and your demise."

The anger raged inside me and I barely kept it in check. I needed him close and sloppy if the plan was going to work.

"What is all this? You're going to find all of the lost runes to do what, become a god?" I said, my voice laced with as much venom as I could summon. It wasn't difficult. "You're pathetic. Who would worship a loser like you?"

"You will never find out," he said, his voice a promise of pain and death. "Take this one to go."

He formed a small white orb in his palm. It was the size of a golf ball but shone like the sun. I looked away, but I felt the energy coming off it in waves. I knew if it hit me directly, I was going to die—at least temporarily.

He released the orb. I manifested Ebonsoul and threw it. I raised my shield. The orb cut right through it and my shoulder. It smashed into the schist and kept going.

<Now, boy!>

William dodged Ebonsoul, letting it sail past him. Peaches blinked out from behind me and reappeared behind William. Peaches caught Ebonsoul by the hilt and did a quick turn, burying the blade in William's leg.

William howled with pain and anger and kicked Peaches across the floor. Peaches somersaulted, crashed into a wall, and bounced a few times. across the marble floor. I held my breath until he stood up and shook it off.

<Can I bite him now?>
<Not yet. Remember the plan.>

<He kicked me. I really want to bite him.>
<Wait. Not yet.>

I felt the siphon from Ebonsoul drain energy from William. Heat flushed my body and healed the hole in my shoulder. He was using the White Heart as a power source and didn't notice what Ebonsoul was doing.

"I'm going to kill you and your aberration of a dog," William said through gritted teeth as he pulled out Ebonsoul and threw it at me. "Then I'll deal with Father's favorite."

I extended my hand and focused. The blade became a silver mist and flowed into my arm. Power surged through me. I kept it under control even though it threatened to burst forth from every pore in my body.

It was time to press buttons. If he was anything like Monty, my next move would completely set him off.

"I know wizards with more power than you," I jeered. "Is that all you got?"

"*Wizards?*" For a second, I thought he was going to burst a blood vessel. "Did you just compare me to wizards?"

"I'd never do that," I said, serious. "I said I know wizards with *more power* than you. Maybe you should go back to Mage School. I'm sure they have a remedial program."

He went ballistic and then calmed down. His energy signature spiked and then flatlined. That was where I needed him to stay.

"I'm going to enjoy killing you. After this I'll head to the Sanctuary with the Gray Heart and raze it to the ground, right after I eviscerate my dear Uncle Dex."

I heard a soft wail behind me and moved to the side.

Monty had recovered and unsheathed the Sorrows.

<Get ready, boy.>

"Give me the White Heart," Monty said, advancing. "Before it's too late."

"Give it to you?" William scoffed. "Who do you think you are to make demands of me? My power dwarfs yours, little Tris."

William lunged forward with his blade. Monty parried the thrust and rotated his body left, unleashing an orb, at William.

William brought his sword up, deflected the orb, and swiped down to cut Monty in an arc. Monty formed a cross block and stopped the descending cut.

William kicked out and connected with Monty's midsection. Monty rolled with the blow and stepped back, avoiding another slash. They circled each other, testing defenses and using feints.

William took two quick steps forward and then slid to the side. Monty saw the move and unleashed a violet orb forcing William to slide back in front of one of the Sorrows. Monty stepped forward and thrust as I pressed my mark.

White light blinded me as the heady smell of lotus blossoms filled my lungs. A complex citrus scent filled the station, a mixture of lemons and oranges. The taste of cinnamon burst in my mouth and the overpowering smell of sweet earth wrapped itself around me a second later. Everything became unfocused and time froze.

"Splinter, you really have grown tired of living," Karma said as she examined the tableau. She was dressed simply in a long white robe that reminded me of the Wordweavers. "Fratricide is a little dark, even for Tristan. Killing a brother never ends well. I usually have to release massive amounts of energy when this happens."

"Hello, Karma," I said. "I'm not going to let Monty kill him."

She stepped closer and examined the Sorrow aimed at William's chest. "Let me guess, you need my help?" she said, pointing at the sword.

"No. I have something to give you."

She narrowed her eyes at me. "What could you possibly give me? Besides your life?"

I pointed at William. "The White Heart," I said. "One of the lost runes."

Karma looked at William and tapped her chin. "Splinter, I'm impressed. At this rate you'll be ready in no time."

"Two conditions," I said, holding up two fingers, and pushing my luck. "Or no deal."

"You realize you're in no position to bargain," Karma said, glancing at me. She had stepped close to William, and I could see she wanted to take the White Heart.

"I disagree," I said, letting my hand graze my mark. "I'm beginning to understand a little more. I'll eventually see the whole picture."

"One could only hope," Karma said. "Very well. What are your conditions?"

"You take the White Heart, erase William's abilities, and don't kill anyone."

"That's three conditions."

"No. The erasure and no killing are the conditions. Your getting the White Heart is the bonus—Deal?"

"And if I refuse?"

I gave her a hard stare. "I keep the White Heart and learn how to use it. Then I'll form the Gray, find the other three lost runes and totally screw up causality for as long as I live. I'll undo every effect to your cause. It will be my life's mission to torment you."

"Or, I could kill you now, take the White Heart, and let these two end each other."

"But you won't," I said, gambling on my life. "You need me."

"You overestimate your importance," she said, flexing her jaw. "I don't *need* anyone."

"You're the one who named me Splinter," I said. "Some things require a small irritant to cause a desired effect."

"'Irritant' perfectly describes you," she answered, and I knew I had her. "I accept your terms, but here is one of my own." She placed a finger in the center of my forehead and images exploded in my mind.

I fell to the ground, dizzy. "What was that?" I asked catching my breath. "What did you do?"

"Something for later," she said, pointing at Monty. "Do you plan on letting him run his brother through?"

I shook my head to clear it and stood unsteadily. I pulled Monty's arm back and pointed him in the other direction. Karma sidled up to William and placed a hand on his chest. White light exploded around her hand. When she removed it from his chest, she held a white stone.

She placed her other hand on his forehead and said something under her breath. A gold cloud enveloped William. She said another word and siphoned the cloud into her hand. She nodded to me, absorbed the White Heart, and disappeared.

Time snapped back into place.

<Now, boy!>

Peaches blinked out and reappeared with his jaws wrapped around William's leg. Monty stabbed the air beside him and turned.

"What did you do?" William asked. "You took my magic?"

He lunged forward and Monty disarmed him easily, tossing the sword to one side.

"I did no such thing," Monty answered and narrowed his eyes. After a few moments, he realized the truth. William had been erased. "It appears you've undergone an erasure. Perhaps overuse of the White Heart."

"Bollocks," William spat back, shaking his leg and failing to remove Peaches. "You did this somehow. Get this infernal creature off me."

"Actually, it was me," I said. "I think it's time for you to retire."

"*You?*" he said. "You insignificant speck of dust. To think that you could defeat *me* is laughable."

"Sometimes the smallest splinter can cause the greatest pain," I said, stepping away from the growing Peaches.

<Hey, boy, change of plans.>

<Can I bite him hard now? He kicked me.>

<No. Do you remember the bad place? With the trolls?>

<Yes.>

<Can you find it?>

<Yes. Can I take him there?>

<When I tell you to.>

"Tristan," William said as Peaches grew, "I promise you vengeance. I will reacquire my ability, and I will destroy you and this sorry excuse of a human."

"You twisted Niall and Gabrielle," I said, shaking my head. "You deserve pain and death, not mercy."

"They were tools to be used, nothing more, nothing less." William struggled against Peaches again but couldn't break free. "The chattel exists to serve a higher purpose. I am that higher purpose."

"Time for you to go," I said. "Take him home, boy."

Peaches blinked out and took William with him.

"Where did you send him?"

"I was going to send him to Dex, but he has his hands full."

"Where did you send him?"

"Same place he was going to leave you to die—the Pit."

"Without magic, the Pit isn't fatal to him," Monty said. "He deserved worse, but I can accept this."

Peaches appeared a few minutes later.

<*Did you bite him?*>

<*No, but I wanted to. I left him where we found the angry man. Do you think he could make some meat?*>

<*I'm positive he'll make you some.*>

TWENTY-NINE

A PORTAL OPENED next to us. TK and LD stepped through, carrying the Black Heart inside a gray orb.

"Good work, Simon," LD said, clapping me on the shoulder. "I'm really glad we didn't have to go nuclear."

"Nuclear?" I asked. "What do you mean nuclear?"

"If William somehow defeated all of you, we would have collapsed the vault," TK said matter-of-factly. "Effectively burying all of the artifacts. Congratulations on your successful shift, Tristan."

Monty gave her a short nod. "Thank you."

"Wouldn't that also bury all of us?" I asked. "What if we were still alive?"

TK nodded. "Sometimes, the needs of the many outweigh the needs of the few," TK said, turning to LD. "Do you recall who said that, Darling?"

"You did, just now, hun," LD answered with a smile, tracing runes and opening another portal.

"Sometimes?" I asked. "What about the other times?"

TK's face darkened and she took a step closer,

lowering her voice. I felt the increase of energy surge around her as she spoke.

"On occasion you will encounter those who can't be reasoned or negotiated with," TK said, placing a hand on my shoulder. "Some just want to watch the world burn. When you encounter them, and you will, you must become unrelenting annihilation. Nothing short of total destruction will slake their thirst. Your job is to make sure the destruction they encounter is their own."

"I'm really glad you didn't go nuclear," I said after a pause. "What are you going to do with the Black Heart?"

"We're going to...You know what? It's better we don't say," LD said. "We have to get back and renovate the Boutique, again. You need anything, you know how to contact us."

"What about the Zombie Queen? We can't let the city get overrun with revenants."

TK nodded. "We're going to coordinate with Erik and the Council to deal with Gabrielle and her undead," she said. "The revenants will be returned to where they belong and Niall will most likely have a cellmate soon."

They stepped through the portal and disappeared.

"Remind me never get on TK's bad side," I said.

Monty nodded. "She would be a formidable opponent, even with my recent shift. I don't think I'd last more than a few minutes against her."

"Can we go home now?" I asked as we headed to the train. "I'd like to take a century off from facing monsters."

"I doubt we'll have the luxury of a century," Monty answered. "Probably closer to a week."

"I'll take a week if it means not dealing with magic, mayhem, and monsters."

"I'd like to go see Roxanne and inform her of my well-being."

"Why don't you take her to Roselli's and have your 'talk' over dinner?" I asked. "I'm sure she'd love that."

"It's almost dawn. Let's drop by the Moscow and I'll set the reservations for this evening."

THIRTY

I PARKED THE Dark Goat in the garage and took the elevator to the lobby. Being that driving the Goat was potentially fatal, I made sure to park it myself when we arrived. The valet still admired it, but I also got the sense he was a little scared of it. The Dark Goat scared people on a visceral level.

I loved that car.

Monty was on the phone, placing the reservations for Roselli's. Peaches sat on his haunches next to me. He rumbled and I saw his ears perk and immediately enter defensive mode. When we stepped into the lobby, my hand was on Grim Whisper, ready for an attack.

Olga stood behind reception and frosted us with one of her glares. She stepped out from behind the enormous desk and motioned for us to follow her to the main office.

"Hello, Olga, you're looking glacial today."

"Ha ha, very funny, Stronk," she said, mangling my name as usual. "I have situation. Now *you* have situation."

"Situation?" I asked. "What kind of situation?"

She pointed to a door on the other side of the office. I walked over and she motioned for me to open it.

"Open, go ahead."

I opened the door, ready for anything. After the last few days of revenants, necromancers, and fearcasting, I was on edge. Nothing prepared me for what I saw on the other side of the door, though.

I looked through the doorway and saw a little girl. She couldn't have been older than ten. She waved at me when I poked my head in. That's when I saw the monster. At least I thought it was a monster until the little girl hugged it. She jumped out of the chair she was sitting in when she saw Peaches.

"He's beautiful!" she said, wrapping her arms around Peaches' neck and looking up at me. "What's his name?"

<Did you hear that? She said I'm beautiful.>

"I did," she said. "You *are* beautiful."

Peaches and I both looked at her.

"Cecelia, go watch your Rags, go, go," Olga said, clapping her hands. "Last time she chew my chairs. My *expensive* chairs."

"I'm sorry, Aunt Olga," Cecelia said and gave Peaches another hug. "Maybe we can be friends?"

I watched her run into the other room and hug her… I wanted to say dog but it was too large to fit that description. Now I knew how people felt when they met Peaches for the first time.

"What kind of dog is that?"

"That is her guardian, Caucasian mountain dog." Olga shook her head. "Still puppy and so huge. Will get bigger, much bigger. Her family sent her to me because of you."

She pointed at Monty.

"Me?" Monty said, flustered. "What do you mean because of me? I don't know who that child is."

"No, but you know mother." Olga crossed her arms and stared at us. "Not look familiar?"

I raised my hands in surrender after a few seconds. "Not really," I said. "Something about her seems familiar, but I don't know anyone who has kids."

"You?" She looked at Monty. "Familiar?"

"Absolutely not," Monty said, staring at Olga. "Why should she be?"

"Her mother is Steigh Cea Styne," Olga said with finality. "Familiar now?"

The memory rushed back. Sky-blue eyes, white-blond hair, psychotic crazy dance behind the eyes—that Steigh Cea Styne. The Stynes were one of the Jotnar entrusted with keeping the runic neutralizer safe. They thrived in ice and cold.

Apparently, some time ago, Monty had to pretend to be engaged to Steigh Cea to complete a mission. Turns out only Monty was pretending, even though he didn't know it at the time.

"This is your fake fiancée's daughter," I said. "Does that mean that you're the—?"

"No," Monty said immediately. "Steigh Cea and I were never intimate. It was a ruse for the mission. I explained this to you."

"And yet here we are with little Steigh Cea in the other room," I said. "I think she has your eyes."

Monty glared at me.

"Olga, why is she here?" Monty asked, pinching the bridge of his nose. "I have no connection to her or her family."

"They send to me because little Cece is special," Olga said, waving her fingers around. "She is like you."

"Like me?" Monty asked. "How?"

"I show," Olga said. "Cece, come here."

The little girl bounded into the room with a smile.

"Yes, Aunty Olga?"

<*She's beautiful.*>

<*She's a young girl. Are you okay?*>

<*I know. I wonder if she likes meat?*>

I looked at Peaches and saw him fixated on the mountain bear dog, which was completely ignoring him.

<*I don't think you're her type.*>

<*She has a type? What kind of type is her type? Do you know? Can you have the angry man make her a sausage, and tell her it's from me?*>

"Show them," Olga said. "Show these men what you can do."

"Are you sure, Aunty?" Cece asked, taking a step back. "Aunty Hekla said I must never show what I can do."

Olga nodded. "I know, but these men are good. They will help you."

Cece looked from Monty to me. "Okay." She nodded. "If you say it's okay."

"Show," Olga said and moved back. She waved Monty and me back. "Show now."

Cece extended her hands and held them there for a few seconds. "Great, she can extend her arms?" I asked. "Most kids her age have mastered this abili—"

I felt the shift in energy the next second and a barrage of icicles shot out from her fingers, burying themselves in the wall across from us.

Olga got on the phone as Monty approached the little girl. "Andrei, we need fix wall in back office," she said and hung up the phone. "You see, she like you."

I don't know what surprised me more. That this little girl was a Jotnar ice mage, or that Olga knew about Monty.

"She's Jotnar," Monty said, looking at Cecelia. "She's a mage?"

"Like mother," Olga answered pulling out an official-looking document from a desk. "Mother say here you teach little girl how to control ice."

"May I see that?" Monty asked. "Where did you get this?"

"Cece, go with Rags," Olga said, agitated. "She chew my chair again. Go, go!"

I looked into the other room and the mountain bear dog-creature was gnawing on one of the arms of the chair. With a shake of its head, it ripped off the arm and tossed it to one side. Cecelia ran in and corrected the large dog-like creature with a finger.

"Rags, no!" I heard before she closed the door.

<Did you see that? How she shredded that chair? She may have hellhound blood.>

<Why don't you just go over there and introduce yourself?>

<I couldn't. Don't you see how amazing she is?>

Olga handed the document to Monty. "I'm to be her magical teacher?"

"She your apprentice now. Paper official with your Golden Circle."

"Whoa, Steigh Cea went through the Golden Circle?"

I looked at the document and there on the bottom was the emblem of the Golden Circle. It was a group of runes surrounded by a—you guessed it—golden circle. No one said mages were creatively inclined.

"No," Monty said, shaking his head. "I've never had an apprentice. I wouldn't know how to teach her. Besides, where would she live?"

"She will live on second floor next to you," Olga said. "Lawyers move up, give entire second floor to me. Cecelia lives there with nanny and guardian monster dog, next to teacher."

"I can't agree to this," Monty said. "If you know who and what I am, then you know she would be in danger."

Olga placed her arms on the table. "You say yes," Olga said as the temperature in the room started dropping. "You and I keep *fridr*, peace. You say no, everyone in building in danger."

Monty remained silent until I could see the frost, emanating from Olga's fingers, creep across the table.

"Monty?" I asked. "I'd really like not to engage the ice-queen building owner in warfare."

"We'll try it for a three-month probationary period," Monty said. "If she doesn't listen to instruction or is unqualified, we end the apprenticeship."

Olga smiled. It was the smile of the person who heard your terms and disregarded them completely.

"Very good," Olga said and stood. "She will be there next week, you start classes. No damage to building."

"What have I started?" Monty said as we left the office. "This is a disaster."

"Does this mean you're a sensei now?"

"Only if you want me to blast you to within an inch of your life," Monty snapped. "I don't know how to teach an apprentice. Much less a little Jotnar girl."

"I'm sure there are books on this sort of thing. Maybe you can contact Professor Ziller?" I asked, suppressing a laugh. "I'm sure Dex would love to help you."

"I'm pleased this is so entertaining for you," he said, opening the door to our office. "Nothing good will come of this, mark my words."

"Yes, sensei," I said with a bow. "Nothing good."

My senses all triggered at once. I drew Grim Whisper and aimed at the figure seated on the sofa in our reception area.

"Corbel," Monty said, absorbing the flame orb he had created, "are you trying to get incinerated?"

"I'm mostly flame-proof."

"You're not entropy bullet-proof," I said, holstering Grim Whisper. "Wait, are you?"

"Do you think I would tell you either way?" Corbel answered. "Don't be dense."

"No, how about you tell us why you're risking your life breaking into our office?"

"I need your help."

"You work for Hades," I said. "I doubt we can out-troubleshoot the god of the Underworld."

"That's just it," Corbel answered. "He can't be seen to be acting on this. It could start another Heavenly War."

"Another?" I asked. "Who won the first one?"

"The big three aren't called that by accident," Corbel said. "This is a delicate matter and Hades requested you by name."

"What is it?" Monty asked.

"She's missing," Corbel said as if we were supposed to know who 'she' was. "She never made it to her scheduled pick up."

"Can you back up a bit?" I asked. "Who's 'she'?"

"Hades' wife."

"I'm drawing a blank," I said, looking at Monty. "Mrs. Hades?"

"Persephone?" Corbel replied, frustrated. "Her name is Persephone."

"What do you mean missing?" Monty asked.

"I mean someone kidnapped Persephone and Hades wants you to find her."

THE END

Cast

Angel Ramirez-Director of the NYTF and friend to Simon Strong. Cannot believe how much destruction one detective agency can wage in the course of one day.

Cecil Fairchild-Owner of SuNaTran and close friend of Tristan Montague. Provides transport for the supernatural community and has been known to make a vehicle disappear in record time.

Dex Montague-Uncle to Tristan, brother to Connor. One of the most powerful mages in the Golden Circle.

Gabrielle- Necromancer and partner to Niall.

Grey Stryder-one of the last Night Wardens patrolling the city and keeping the streets safe. Current owner of *Kokutan no ken*.

Kali-(AKA Divine Mother) goddess of Time, Creation, Destruction, and Power. Cursed Simon for unspecified reasons and has been known to hold a grudge. She is also one of the most powerful magic-users in existence.

Karma-The personification of causality, order, and balance. She reaps what you sow. Also known as the mistress of bad timing. Everyone knows the saying karma is a…some days that saying is true.

Kragzimik-Ancient type of dragon whose purpose is to rid the world of non-dragon magic-users. Much like every dragon. Really despises mages and magic-users.

LD Tush Rogue Creative Mage, husband to TK Tush. Proprietor of Fordey Boutique. One of the Ten.

Mark Ronin-Division 13 agent currently on extended leave.

Michiko Nakatomi-(AKA 'Chi' if you've grown tired of breathing) Vampire leader of the Dark Council. Reputed to be the most powerful vampire in the Council.

The Morrigan-Yes *that* Morrigan. Chooser of the Slain and currently in a relationship with Uncle Dex...don't ask. Also goes by Badb Catha the 'Boiling One.'

Niall- Pavormancer who specializes in fearcasting and using fear against his opponents.

Noh Fan Yat- Martial arts instructor for the Montague & Strong Detective Agency. Teacher to both Simon and Tristan. Known for his bamboo staff of pain and correction.

Peaches-(AKA Devildog, Hellhound, Arm Shredder

and Destroyer of Limbs) Offspring of Cerberus and given to the Montague & Strong Detective Agency to help with their security. Closely resembles a Cane Corso-a very large Cane Corso.

Professor Ziller Mage responsible for the safeguarding of the Living Library and the Repository of knowledge at the Golden Circle. Don't try to have conversation with him…it will just melt your brain.

Roxanne DeMarco-Director of Haven. Oversees both the Medical and Detention Centers of the facility. Is an accomplished sorceress with formidable skill. Has been known to make Tristan stammer and stutter with merely a touch of his arm.

Simon Strong-The intelligent (and dashingly handsome) half of the Montague & Strong Detective Agency. Cursed alive into immortality by the goddess Kali.

TK Tush Rogue Creative Mage, wife to LD Tush. Proprietor of Fordey Boutique. One of the Ten. She's not angry…really.

Tristan Montague- The civilized (and staggeringly brilliant) half of the Montague & Strong Detective Agency. Mage of the Golden Circle sect and currently on 'extended leave' from their ever-watchful supervision.

William Montague-Older brother to Tristan. Dark Mage and teacher of Niall and Gabrielle

Wordweavers- An ancient sect of magic-users. They manipulate magic through speech and special words of power. Considered to be the first magic-users.

<u>ORGANIZATIONS</u>

Fordey Boutique- Artifact specialty store dealing in rare magical items that are usually dangerous and lethal, like the owners

New York Task Force-(AKA the NYTF) a quasi-military police force created to deal with any supernatural event occurring in New York City.

Sheol-Magical supermax prison.

SuNaTran-(AKA Supernatural Transportations) Owned by Cecil Fairchild. Provides car and vehicle service to the supernatural community in addition to magic-users who can afford membership.

The Dark Council-Created to maintain the peace between humanity and the supernatural community shortly after the last Supernatural War. Its role is to be a check and balance against another war occurring. Not everyone in the Council favors peace.

The Ten-A clandestine group of magic-users and shifters whose purpose is to…well that's secret now isn't it?

<u>Special Mentions for Bullets &</u>

<u>Blades</u>

Niall- Pronounced like the river. Pavormancy is nasty stuff and playing with people's fears is just plain wrong…you deserve everything that happened… you're welcome.

<u>Just going to call this the Tushs' Section</u>

<u>Thank you Larry and Tammy:</u>

For Deathane…never feed a hellhound broccoli… ever.

Sometimes meat can be unlife lol. Ask Peaches.

Some people do walk around with a nimbus of fury.

For providing the triage decision tree to help those who were damaged in the making of this book.

It's bad when the stupid burns in advance.

Because we don't kick ass. We engage in extremely percussive gluteal impacts.

Glen V. because the **javambrosia** DeathWish Coffee coupon wouldn't exist without you. Thanks to you, we can all… "Stay caffeinated. My friends."

Cecelia- because you wanted to be in a book.

Looking forward to your own stories soon.

AUTHOR NOTES

Thank you for reading this story and jumping back into the world of Monty & Strong.

Fear isn't real and yet we are all touched by it at some point in our lives. It certainly feels real when it has us in its grip, but if we think about it, we create our fears. This is why everyone experiences fear differently. Some fear is healthy and some not so much. I would still want to blowtorch a tarantula if it crawled into bed with me. Wouldn't you?

Simon went through some fear in this book. By putting him through this, I was able to face why we fear and what causes us to fear. Usually the cause of the fear is greater than the thing we fear. It's just that sometimes it's hard to tell the difference. Thank you for allowing me to deal with those feelings when I wrote this story.

With each book, I want to introduce you to different elements of the world Monty & Strong inhabit, slowly revealing who they are and why they make the choices they do. If you want to know how they met, that story is in NO GOD IS SAFE, which is a short, explaining how Tristan and Simon worked their first case.

There are some references you will understand and

some…you may not. This may be attributable to my age (I'm older than Monty, or feel that way most mornings) or to my love of all things sci-fi and fantasy. As a reader, I've always enjoyed finding these "Easter Eggs" in the books I read. I hope you do too. If there is a reference you don't get, feel free to email me and I will explain it…maybe.

You will notice that Simon is still a smart-ass (deserving a large head smack) and many times he's clueless about what's going on. He's also acquired more spells (an anemic magic missile and undead sausage) even though he needs some practice. He's slowly wrapping his head around the world of magic, but it's a vast universe and he has no map.

Bear with him—he's still new to the immortal, magical world he's been delicately shoved into. Fortunately he has Monty to nudge (or blast) him in the right direction.

Each book will reveal more about Monty & Strong's backgrounds and lives before they met. Rather than hit you with a whole history, I wanted you to learn about them slowly, the way we do with a person we just met—over time (and many large cups of DeathWish Coffee).

Thank you for taking the time to read this book. I wrote it for you and I hope you enjoyed spending a few more hours getting in (and out of) trouble with

Tristan and Simon.

If you really enjoyed this story, I need you to do me a **HUGE** favor— **Please leave a review**.

It's really important and helps the book (and me). Plus, it means Peaches gets new titanium chew toys, besides my arms, legs, and assorted furniture to shred. And I get to keep him at normal size (most of the time).

We want to keep Peaches happy, don't we?

Contact me:

I really do appreciate your feedback. Let me know what you thought by emailing me at:
www.orlando@orlandoasanchez.com

For more information on Monty & Strong...come join the MoB Family on Facebook!

You can find us at:

Montague & Strong Case Files.

To get **FREE** stories visit my page at:

www.orlandoasanchez.com

Still here? Amazing! Well, if you've made it this far
—you deserve something special!

Included is the first chapter of the next Montague &
Strong story-HELL HATH NO FURY here for you to
read.

Enjoy!

ı

HELL HATH NO FURY

A Montague and Strong Detective Agency Book 8

ONE

"What do you mean kidnapped?" I asked.

Corbel reached into a pocket and produced two medium-sized sausages. He tossed one to Peaches, who caught and inhaled it in one bite.

<Why didn't you let me know he was there? I almost shot him.>

<He isn't a bad man. He smells like home and he has meat.>

"He's getting big." Corbel rubbed Peaches' head as my hellhound chomped on the second sausage he fed him.

"Who would kidnap Hades' wife?"

Corbel stared at me. "That's the first intelligent question you've asked," he said, rubbing his face. "I don't know who would be suicidal enough to make this move against Hades."

"Where was she?" Monty asked. "You said she never made it to her scheduled pick up. Pick up from where?"

"At her home."

"Not the underworld?" I asked. "Isn't that where she lives?"

"Persephone spends a large portion of her time on this plane," Corbel answered. "Their relationship is *complex*."

"She has a home here?" Monty asked. "In the city?"

Corbel nodded. "Midtown, off Central Park West."

"Does anyone know where this alleged kidnapping took place?" I asked. "Was she home?"

"No. Security is too tight. What do you mean *alleged*?" Corbel asked. "She was taken."

"Have you met Hades? He is the god of the Underworld, not exactly mister cheerful and romance. Maybe she wanted something different in her life. Maybe a place with a little sun?"

"Are you implying she *left* him?" Corbel asked, flexing his jaw. "She would never leave him."

"Wouldn't leave him, or *can't* leave him?" I asked, wiggling my fingers. "Maybe Hades worked some spell on her?"

"Their relationship is *complex*," Corbel said with a sigh. "No, she wasn't compelled to remain with him."

"Complex? Is that code for she couldn't stand him?"

"Complex," he said, glaring at me. "Like the one an immortal detective might have with an ancient vampire."

"Ouch, no need to get sensitive. Just asking the basic questions."

"If you ask him those questions, prepare for pain."

"Just noting that they spent time apart," I answered. "Did she care for him?"

Corbel glared at me. "She and Hades have an understanding. They take regular time away from each other."

"Does he love her? Or does he go around Zeusafying every woman he sees, making little demigods?"

"He loves her," Corbel said with finality. "He wouldn't subject me to the torture of speaking to you if he didn't."

I nodded. "Right, so she was kidnapped or ran away."

"For your self-preservation, I'm going to suggest you

refrain from expressing that opinion around Hades when you meet him."

"Meet him? We literally just got home. Can you give us a moment to at least change clothes?"

"No. Hades wants you on this now."

"Before we go see your boss, we should see her place," I said. "Maybe there's something there that will let us know who is behind this. Maybe a boyfriend?"

Corbel shook his head and looked at Monty. "How do you work with him?"

"Tea and patience," Monty said. "Copious amounts of both.

38374009R00163

Made in the USA
Middletown, DE
07 March 2019